FOR WHOM THE SPELL TOLLS

Come for the readings...stay for the revenge...

Jules Larkwood, a witch looking for a little adventure, doesn't expect her friendly bet with the town's oldest vampire to change her life. Then a powerful enemy from her past rises from the dead, and Jules' life becomes a little *too* interesting.

Now she must juggle tracking down ancient spells, thwarting secret rituals, and facing old foes, while attending her book club and keeping her crystal shop open for Ordinary's full moon festival.

But when a woman is found dead, all bets are off. Jules and her best friends Medusa (yes, that Medusa) and a seer named Piper, are on the hunt, and running out of time to catch the murderer before the next victim falls...

FOR WHOM THE SPELL TOLLS

ORDINARY OREGON MYSTERY
BOOK 2

DEVON MONK

ODD
HOUSE
PRESS

For my Family

CHAPTER 1

"The mirror." The vampire casually leaned one elbow on the counter. "Is it for sale?"

Old Rossi was the head of all the vampires who lived here in Ordinary, Oregon. That sounded like a big, powerful job (and I supposed it might be, *sometimes*), but as far as I could tell, Rossi spent his time sticking his nose into other people's business and gossiping at his yoga studio.

"Hmmm," I said. "Of which mirror are you speaking?"

His eyes narrowed.

I grinned.

"Jules."

"Rossi."

"You are a witch. A very powerful witch."

"I am the most powerful witch in town."

He tipped his head to one side. "Well, technically..."

"Nope. Not technically. I am the most powerful. I might look like I'm in my thirties..."

He hummed and rocked his head to the other side.

I fake gasped. "I might look," I said louder, "like I'm in my thirties, but I am a woman in her seventies—in her prime. And brother, I can out-spell anyone, anytime, anywhere."

"When you're not trying to catch murderers."

Nose in *everyone's* business.

"One time. I helped catch a murderer one time! And it wasn't just me. Dusi figured it out before I did. But if a *new* murderer came to town? You bet your fangs I'd find them before anyone else."

His ice-blue eyes flashed with interest. "I'll take that bet. How about we put something interesting on the line?"

I went back to arranging the Tarot charms hanging on the countertop spinner. The latest shipment were little hand-painted wooden cards. I adored them. "Like there's ever going to be another murder in this town."

He waited. Vampires were patient. Ancient vampires (like Rossi) could outwait the heat death of the universe.

"You aren't allowed to murder someone," I said.

He snorted. "If I did, no one would ever know."

"Rossi."

"Jules." He grinned, flashing just a bit of fang. "I've lived here longer than you. I know the rules."

"All right. *If* there is ever another murder in town...*If,*" I insisted.

He dipped his chin, encouraging me to go on.

"I will bet you a particularly rare, magical compact mirror that I will find the murderer."

"Before Delaney or the rest of the police," he said.

"Yes, before the police or anyone else solves the case."

Saying that sent a tingle of excitement down my spine. Solving the murder with Dusi and Piper last month had been fun. But I hadn't realized until now how much I wanted more of that kind of challenge.

I mean, yes, I wanted to win this bet, but I loved puzzles, mysteries, and solving problems. I loved helping people. It made me feel like I had a purpose, a north star to follow.

But giving a certain old vampire a run for his money (or for the mirror he'd wanted me to sell him for years) made me wish someone would drop dead outside my shop right now.

I mean, not really, but also kind of really.

"What do I get when you lose?" I asked.

He gave me a charming smile that could make a person want to drop to their knees and ask for more.

"Rossi," I said, very much not dropping to my knees. "What do I get?"

"I've mentioned I have some...unique crystals and stones, haven't I?"

Once, when he was really drunk, he'd specifically told me he had stones that were so rare, their match didn't exist on earth.

"You have."

"I will open the vault and allow you to take whichever stone your heart desires."

"I suppose that will be after you remove all the really valuable ones."

"Please. There's no fun in it if I cheat—it kills the thrill. All stones will be there for your choosing."

Another tingle ran down my spine—anticipation. He'd once (yes, that same drunken night) rambled on about how powerful some of those crystals and stones were. They'd be an amazing complement to my magic without breaking the rules of me not tapping into Ordinary's big magic when I used witchcraft.

But I liked that mirror. I liked keeping it because I didn't know what it could really do, and I didn't know why Rossi really wanted it.

However, the chances of a murder happening in Ordinary was zip plus zero.

Which meant this bet was just for fun.

"All right, Rossi." I held out my hand, and we shook, charms and bracelets on my wrist chiming softly. "You've got a bet. The next time a murder happens in Ordinary, I'll solve it before the police."

"Let's hear it for crimes of passion," he said. "May they be ample and devious."

I wagged my finger. "Don't let Delaney here you talking like that."

He zipped his jacket and flipped up the collar. "Delaney adores me. I'll let you know if I hear of any terrible accidental deaths, wink-wink."

"You won't have to, because I'll already be on the scene, wink-wink."

The bell over the shop door rang out, and a tourist wandered in. She wiped her wet shoes on the mat and pushed back the hood of her puffy coat, then started browsing the mystical items on the shelves to her right.

Rossi gave me a nod, slipped his sunglasses on, and strode out into the rainy March day.

It wasn't that I *wanted* a crime to happen. But the reason I'd built my crystal and Tarot shop—the Fool Moon—here over thirty years ago was because of the town. It was one of the only places in the world where gods put down their powers to vacation and plenty of supernaturals lived right alongside humans.

It was the perfect set up for all sorts of shenanigans.

But had any shenanigans happened today?

No.

Yesterday?

Nope.

The last four weeks? Nada.

Even Delaney Reed, who was like a daughter to me (and who was also the Chief of Police) hadn't asked for my help with anything lately.

All the normalness was making me restless.

I'd already counted inventory three times, double checked all my outstanding orders, and dealt out so many random Tarot readings for myself, I was starting to play solitaire with the cards.

Which was probably why I'd just made a stupid bet with a vampire.

After a few minutes, the tourist wandered out of the store. I locked the door behind her.

I tugged the star curtains across the front window and flipped the OPEN sign to CLOSED.

Not a moment too soon.

Three slow, foreboding knocks rattled the back door. I wasn't psychic like my friend Piper, but I knew who was on my doorstep.

Death.

The knocks thumped again, slow as a heart's last beat.

"Hold your pale horses, Than." I waved my hands, bracelets jangling, and sent magic skipping across the shop to tidy up, turn down the music, and flick on the twinkling lights.

The crystals, Tarot, and enchanted statues glittered —stones and mystic items catching and returning the lowered light like a happy whispered secret. A little fountain in the back corner quietly burbled mermaid dreams, and I couldn't help but smile.

I loved this place. It was almost too small now, since I'd been adding more inventory and shelves over the years, but I couldn't imagine not having my shop and the life I'd built with it.

I strolled to the back room where I'd stacked boxes of extra stock to one side to make room for the couches and chairs that created a cozy sitting area. The small kitchenette was already set with snacks and beverages for everyone.

Even though he had put down his power in order to

vacation in Ordinary, the god of death outside my door projected a *presence*.

Well, the god of death could wait a couple seconds more. I patted my hair, which I'd left unbound today because the curl was amazing, and smoothed my swishy green and blue skirts (spring colors were my favorite) over my hips.

Okay. Show time. Let the fun begin.

I opened the door.

Thanatos (Than) was tall and thin, his expression severely neutral, if you ignored the curious glint in his eyes.

He wore an electric blue sweater knit in a pattern telling the story of a ship. The ship sailed over waves, then got stuck in a hole. Then...from the little x's over its sail eyes it...died?

Then it exploded.

Just row after knitted row of the ship blowing into bits, little exploded people and fish splatting all around.

"Jules," he said in a tone that made me think of bottomless canyons, empty voids, and, well, ships exploding into bits. "You look *well* today."

"Thank you." I tossed the rose-gold scarf over my shoulder and stepped aside. "That's a very dramatic sweater, Than."

"Yes." He strolled into the room and moved toward the tea station. "It is."

"Do you know why Xtelle called the emergency book club meeting?" I asked.

"I do not." He lifted a cup and saucer and drew them

toward his face to study their quality. "But I can assume she has some complaint…"

"Wait!" a voice called. "Hold that door."

A pink pony-sized unicorn wearing a shiny silver beret, a silver cape, and blue lipstick galloped toward me, skidding to a stop at the door.

"Was I seen?" she asked breathlessly, craning her neck to look over her rump. "Did you see cameras? Was I spotted?"

"It's Monday, Xtelle." I waved her into the room. "Everyone is working. No one is paying attention to you."

"They *should*. I mean, look at me!" She flounced toward the love seat and turned a circle, tail swishing. "I. Am. Perfection."

"How many times has Delaney told you not to walk around looking like a unicorn?" I asked.

"Who did what?"

"You know who. And you know she enforces the magic laws in town. I've heard her tell you multiple times not to trot about town looking like a pink unicorn."

"I'll have you know I wasn't trotting," she said airily. "I was *cantering*. Magnificently."

She scrambled up onto the loveseat and tilted her head back, her long neck stretched over the armrest. She looked boneless, like a wilted, dying pink flower with blue lips. "Bring me tea and cookies."

"Self-serve only," I said. "And don't say you can't do it. You're the most self-serving person in this town."

Than made a sound of approval.

Xtelle blew air through her horsey lips, covering a laugh. "You are such a witch."

"Thank you."

"Jules!"

Piper and Medusa—Dusi—made their way across the parking area. Dusi wore sunglasses, slacks, and a quilted vest over a sweater. A pink beanie with the Puffin Muffin logo covered her snake hair. Her sunglasses reflected the cloudy sky, but she smiled that almost shy smile of hers.

Medusa was, well, *Medusa*, and had recently moved back to town.

"Hi, Jules," she said.

"Hey, Dusi. How's the house painting going?"

"Good, but not done yet."

Piper waved behind her. She wore wide-legged pants with big flowers at the hem and a soft blue sweater she'd designed and knitted, under a light windbreaker. Her blonde hair was pulled back in a simple ponytail that made her gray eyes seem even wider.

Piper was a demi-god, the child of a god and a mortal. She could see the future, or at least some of the futures. She waitressed at the Blue Owl, a 24/7 diner outside town that did a brisk business with locals, truckers, and passers-through. With her clairvoyant ability, no one's coffee ever went cold, and she never showed up at a table to ask about the meal when someone's mouth was full.

She, and now Dusi, were my best friends.

"I'm glad you both made it." I opened my arms wide and gave them each a hug in turn. "Come in before it starts raining again. You know where the tea is. Help yourself." I scanned the parking area. "Is this everyone?"

"I think Sage and Fawn will be here," Piper said.

"Is that a…" I wiggled my fingers and eyebrows.

Piper laughed. "I'm clairvoyant, but hey, look at this neat trick! Phone with text!" She hung her jacket on the hook by the door. "So, what's the big emergency?"

"We've been betrayed!" Xtelle crowed. She rose like a thing from the dead and narrowed her eyes, teeth bared. "Stabbed in the back. Defied. Today we declare war!"

Than settled into the corner chair, a delicate china cup—the best one I owned—balanced between his long fingers. "War?" His dark eyes glittered.

"No wars." Dusi said as she finished making a cup of hot cocoa. She moved fluidly to the couch and sat. "I've had enough of those. We all have."

"War isn't even allowed in Ordinary," Piper added.

I got my favorite cup (shaped like a cauldron) out of the cupboard and chose the jasmine tea. "Did you have a point, Xtelle?"

"War *is* the point! Someone bring me tea. I am parched."

"No," we all said simultaneously.

"Traitors," she hissed, swiveling her head to spear us all with a look. If that ex-demon queen could actually shoot daggers out of her eyes, we'd have been cold cuts.

I chuckled and Piper slapped her hand over her mouth.

"You are all terrible." She clambered off the divan and primly trotted over to the tea, muttering actual curses under her breath.

"No dark magic in my home," I warned. "And really? None in Ordinary, you know that."

"Oopsie!" Xtelle knocked the sugar bowl onto the floor. "So clumsy."

"One more "oopsie" gets you kicked out of my house."

"Please, I am a *delight*." She stood on her back hooves and poured a cup of coffee before adding an obscene amount of cream to it. "Do clean that up, dear," she ordered.

I shook my head, already on my way to the broom I kept in the corner. A knock at the door made me pause.

"Yep!" Piper popped up out of her chair. "How about I get the broom? You should get the door."

There was something about her smile, something about the twinkle in her eyes that said she knew something I didn't know.

"All right," I said slowly. "You are totally up to something. This better be good." I opened the door and gasped. I hustled to pull the door mostly shut behind me, hiding the pink unicorn from view.

Because there, right there, alive, and handsome, and real, was a man I hadn't seen for decades. A man who had once meant the world to me. Who had once been the only future I had eyes for.

A man I never thought I'd see again.

"West?" I breathed, afraid he was nothing but candlelight wavering in the wind.

"Jules?" He blinked, surprised. The smile lit his deep blue eyes with that mix of good humor and challenge that was a hot elixir. He was summer—the warmth, the intoxication, the ease.

He was also my weakness.

"I didn't know," he said. "I wondered. Wondered if this was yours, the Fool Moon. Your token."

"You." I fluttered my hand at him. "You're here."

I sounded like a teen instead of someone who had one foot firmly in my seventies, even if outwardly I looked half that age.

West was my age but looked to be in his early fifties.

And goddess, didn't his fifties look magnificent on him?

The short beard, the long dark hair he hadn't bothered to tie back, the lines at the corners of his eyes that spoke of a life of laughter. A thin gold chain wrapped around a sturdy leather cord just above the collar of his dark blue flannel jacket made me wonder if it still held his token from all those years ago.

It was impossible not to remember a much younger West through the eyes and emotions of a much younger me.

He had been my tomorrow. What was he doing in my today?

I huffed a laugh, untangling from the sudden onslaught of memories.

"Why are you here?" I asked. "Is something wrong?"

"No, I'm…"

A car door slammed. Fawn (werewolf) and Sage (vampire) jogged toward us.

West turned to let them by.

"Hey, Jules." Fawn glanced at West and promptly ignored him in the way only a disinterested werewolf could. "Meeting started yet?"

"Not yet. Come on in. You, too, Sage," I added.

The vampire had stopped outside the door, but instead of dismissing West, she made a point to frankly assess him.

"Who are you?" she asked. She wore a sweater dress with dark tights and boots that laced up to her knees. In the rainy light, her almost-white hair glowed.

"West," he said, offering his hand. "West Heath."

"Hello, West Heath." Sage shook his hand, then turned to me. "I thought this was a private meeting."

There was more to what she was saying. There was some: *Who is this guy* and a little *What is he doing here,* and a lot of *Who is he to you?*

I liked Sage. She was a great paramedic and had a thing for board games—finding new ones, playing them, and winning. She always had her finger on the pulse of the town and was fun to be around.

But right now, she was giving me a look that said she wasn't sold on whatever she saw in West.

"I didn't mean to interfere," West said, taking a step backward.

I wanted to reach out to him, to catch his hand and

hold him here until he told me why he'd come. Why he'd found me after all these years.

But he hadn't been in my life for decades. A little more time without him wouldn't matter, would it?

"It's a private meeting," I said.

His gaze flicked to the slice of room he could see over my shoulder, curiosity setting fire to his smile.

"Sure," he said. "I can see that. Sorry for just dropping in like this. Maybe we could catch up? Before I leave town?"

Ah. So this was temporary, him being here.

Still, the *yes* and *please* was in me, right there on the tip of my tongue. I ignored them.

I'd learned—from him—that sometimes it was better for your heart to not get what it wanted.

"Stop in during business hours if you want," I said. The breeze picked up, and it was cool and fresh against my hot skin.

"Good," he said. "Yes. See you soon."

I nodded, though I wasn't sure I could do this again, see him again. Wasn't sure I wanted to.

He turned and that familiar stride, the line of his shoulders with the angle of his hips, made my heart flutter. He paused and turned back to face me.

"It's great to see you, Jules. Really great."

I took a breath, then took another to settle my resolve. What was it about him that unspooled everything in me?

Love, my heart said. But I was old enough to ignore that, too.

I stepped inside and shut the door.

Everyone stared at me.

"Ooooh," Xtelle cooed. "Somebody's got a boyfriend *and* a sordid past! Did he cheat on you? Did you cheat on him? Did you cheat *with* each other *on* each other?"

She had produced a bag of popcorn from out of thin air and was nibbling kernels, eyes wide.

"So, the meeting you called today," I said. "Who betrayed us and why do you want to start a war?"

For a moment, I didn't think the group would move on from West. Then Xtelle shoved the popcorn to the side.

"I didn't start it. The war has already been declared! But I'm going to *end* it."

"Who declared war?" I asked.

"Those goons who took our meeting room."

"At the library?" Dusi asked.

"Which goons?" Piper cut in, handing me my tea. She touched my arm gently, reminding me I was still standing by the door, still in shock over seeing West. "There are so many in town." She sat on the couch next to Dusi.

"The most villainous goons of all," Xtelle said ominously.

Thunder rumbled outside.

Than's eyebrows raised. "Xtelle."

The thunder cut off mid-clap.

Fawn, who had prowled the perimeter of the room once before settling in a fold-out chair, blew over the top of her cup. "We could take turns guessing, but I don't have all day."

"Spill it, pony," Sage said.

Xtelle opened her mouth, then closed it. She tossed her head and the silver beret flopped over one eye. "None of you. Not *one* of you has any sense of dramatic timing."

Fawn made a wrap-it-up gesture. Her fingernails were almost claw-length, which made sense. The full moon was Saturday. She'd be running with her pack soon.

"Fine!" Xtelle huffed. "It's the gamer goons. Those treacherous, ratfink twerps."

"Gamers?" I asked. "The gamers Marty hosts aren't twerps."

"Can agree we are not," Sage said lifting her cup toward me. "Also we'd love a few extra hours in the shop next week if that's okay. I got my hands on COSMIC ENCOUNTER, and it's gonna rock."

"Not you *people*," Xtelle growled. "The *Scrabble* Club."

"The Scrabble Club?" Dusi asked.

"Treacherous, ratfink twerps," she repeated.

A knock at the door interrupted the confused silence.

"Aren't we popular today?" I glanced at Piper to see if she knew who it was because I didn't know if I could take another blast from my past.

She shook her head slightly, her eyebrows knitted.

Okay. Not a lot of precognitive help there. But Piper only sees some of the possibilities of the future, not all of the possibilities.

Maybe we were entering a foggy sort of future.

As long as there was some excitement in the fog, I was here for it.

I opened the door. "Sorry, this is a..."

"Jules? It *is* you!" Clara Park, my old rival and sworn enemy, slapped me on the shoulder with a real estate sales brochure and bullied her way past me into the room.

CHAPTER 2

"Wait!" I spun, grasping for Clara, but the witch was too fast. She stopped in the middle of the room, hands on her hips like a head cheerleader assessing the new recruits.

"What are we all up to today?" she asked with saccharin sweetness. She was at least five years older than me but had used magic to keep her appearance in her twenties. Very early twenties.

She was a white-blonde, dewy faced, baby-doll, with peachy cheeks and lips, her eyes just slightly too large. The whole of it made her look even younger.

The lacy ice-blue, mid-thigh dress and strappy white sandals were stupid choices for the rainy, muddy March weather. But Clara was winter, always choosing cold colors to accent her pale complexion.

It was her wrist that caught my eye. It sparkled with gold and silver bracelets, one of which held a single round silver token imprinted with an image of the world on one side and a star on the other. It was the token that held her magic, represented by her Tarot arcana of choice.

I wanted her to be a hallucination, a trick, a nightmare, but she was all too real.

Clara was here. Clara, who I hadn't seen in decades. Clara, who had pushed her way to the top of our class by stomping all over my life and dreams.

Clara, who had proven love would never be in the cards for me.

I tried to speak but couldn't set anchor to my thoughts in the stream of anxiety rushing through my mind.

Was this a panic attack? I hadn't had a panic attack since...well, since Clara.

"Why," Xtelle snarled, "are you interrupting our private meeting?"

Xtelle now appeared to be a devastatingly beautiful woman wearing a black tunic and slacks, her dark hair in a loose braid over one shoulder, her eyes absolutely on fire.

"How cute! You must be Juley's friends." Clara's words dripped sugar. Poisoned sugar. "How *nice* for her."

"Juley?" Dusi's tone indicated she was *this close* to making some serious eye-contact.

I hated the nickname she'd given me back when we were students of the Head Witch Burgess Carmichael. I was angry, but couldn't help but laugh. That had been *years* ago.

"No. We are not doing this," I said. "It's just Jules. It's

always been just Jules." I grabbed Clara's arm. "You need to leave."

Hatred seared across her face so quickly, I wasn't sure I saw it.

Clara stuck out her bottom lip. "You missed me, I know you missed me." She yanked her arm out of my grip.

"Your life is so boring," she said. "You know I *always* have something exciting going on. I came here to give you an exclusive invite. It will be fun. Pinky swear." She held up her pinky.

"No. Whatever it is, no thank you." I pointed at the open door. "Out, please." It was starting to rain, a light, foggy drizzle. "Good-bye."

Clara's sigh was long. She opened her purse, shoved the brochure into it and closed it again. "Well, you are missing out. When you come to your senses, give me a call." She snapped a business card out of thin air. (Yes, magic.)

She handed it to me and leaned in.

"Your life *is* boring, Juley," she whispered, "because you never take risks. You know how much fun we have together. Take a risk. It'll be fun."

She patted my arm and strutted to the door.

"Adieu, friends of Juley. Enjoy your little meeting!" She walked out without shutting the door behind her.

The room was so silent, I wondered if someone had punched the mute button on the reality.

I had an old invisibility spell hidden away in my

guest closet. Right now, I was wishing I'd swallowed it down.

Than cleared his throat. "Yes. Shall we then?"

Piper and Dusi stood, Piper guiding me to a chair, Dusi closing the door and setting the lock.

Piper put my tea in my hands.

"I didn't know," she said. "I'm sorry. I know you are—"

"I'm fine," I said.

She grinned. "Sorry about that. Got my now and then mixed up. She's gone. We're all glad she's gone."

Piper's warmth was like a hug. I shook my head.

"Sorry, everyone. I can't believe I let that woman walk in here. It won't happen again."

"No apologies," Dusi said. "She barged in uninvited."

Nods all around, which made me feel better.

"Hello?" Xtelle had shifted back into her pink unicorn self. She pointed her hoof at each of us in turn. "The Scrabblers? The goons? The war in which we will *destroy* them?" She shook her hoof like a fist in the air.

The Scrabble Club consisted of maybe eight people—all normals—who played the game like some people played slots: with conviction, rigor, and spite.

"How did they take our meeting room from us?" Sage asked. "Don't we book it a week in advance?"

"We do." Fawn picked at her tooth with her pinky. "I booked it. It must be a misunderstanding. Why would the library give it to them?"

"Because they are underhanded sneaky liars, deceivers, and cheats," Xtelle said.

"I'll just reserve it for next time." Fawn shrugged.

"Ha!" Xtelle laughed. "They booked *our* room for the next *six* months."

"Six months?" Fawn tipped her head and I was reminded she was part of the powerful werewolf family in town who could (theoretically) cause a lot of trouble.

"They have beaten us to the punch!" Xtelle wailed. "Where will we discuss the prequel to *Wicked Whoa*? Where will we argue over the literary contributions *Sinful Saddles* brings to the romantic horse genre? This horrifying injustice stands in the way of our horse-centered book discussions."

"And the other books we're reading," Dusi said.

"What books?" Xtelle demanded.

"The mystery? The fantasy? That nonfiction for next week?" Dusi said.

"Yes, yes. But most importantly, the horse books."

"I've been meaning to nominate several more non-horse books," Sage said, unable to resist stirring the pot.

"No!" Xtelle snapped. "We have too many of those. We must focus on reclaiming our territory. Formulate our sneak attack. Vanquish our foes!"

She glanced at Death. "Than, make yourself useful and smite them."

Than stilled. I held my breath. He wasn't a vengeful person, or at least he hadn't behaved that way while he was in town. But one never knew what the god of death might do.

"Perhaps I have been slacking in my reserve officer duties," he intoned.

"Yes. *Yes!*" Xtelle said.

"Such as allowing a demon queen to appear as a unicorn in public instead of insisting she be relocated, permanently, outside of town."

His tone hadn't changed, but who needed thunder when the god of death threatened?

Xtelle opened her mouth, then shut it. "Fine. So, the sneak attack…"

"There will be no sneak attacks," I said. "Fawn, can you check in with the library and explain the situation?"

"I can."

"Good," I said. "How about we meet here until this gets straightened out? It will be tight quarters but should work until we find something else. We'll just have to make sure we don't double book with Marty's board game group because then there really won't be enough room for us all."

"We could invite Marty," Piper said. "That would be nice, right Dusi?"

Dusi took a sip of her cocoa to hide the flush that turned her cheeks pink. I knew she had a crush on my nephew, but the two of them seemed to be doing everything they could not to avoid talking to each other.

It was like they were both playing hard to get and hoping the other would notice. Which was cute, but it had been a month already. Someone needed to start playing easy to get.

Maybe the meetings here would help them start a casual conversation. From the way Marty looked at Dusi, and from the way Dusi looked at him (when he wasn't watching), I could see there was a spark between them.

"Yes to meeting here," Sage said. "And we should totally invite Marty to be a part of the group."

"Thirded," Piper agreed. "You have nice teas, Jules, and the couches are more comfy than the chairs at the library."

"Whoa, hold on, hold on," Xtelle said. "We will *not* simply give up that easily. We will not allow the *Scrabblers* of all people to yank the room out from under our hooves. We have pride. We have dignity. We have rights—more than they do. More rights, I say. More!"

"We do not have more right to a public meeting space," Than said.

"But, war…" The pink unicorn crossed her hooves over her chest. "We could have had a *war*, Than, you big stick in the mud."

"I'll talk to the library and let you all know what they say," Fawn said.

"Good," I said. "We can all look for other meeting spaces too. Any other questions?"

"I have one," Sage said, setting her coffee down and folding her slender, pale fingers together. Piper was giving her don't-do-it eyes, but Than seemed keenly interested. "Who's West," she asked, "and are you as in love with him as he is obviously in love with you?"

CHAPTER 3

A wave of panic prickled down my spine, but these were my friends. I could be honest with them.

"He's just a witch I knew. We were part of a small group who learned magic together. He is very much not in love with me."

Now, I thought as I sipped tea, barely tasting it.

"Uh, huh." Sage's intense vampiric focus might have been unsettling if I didn't know her. "And?"

"We dated." I shook my head at the simplicity of that statement. I'd loved him with all my heart. I'd built my world and future around him.

Then he'd left me.

For Clara.

"That chapter of my life is over and out. You heard him, he's just passing through and saw the sign on my store. He happened to stop by, no big deal, the end."

Everyone was silent. Too silent.

"I see," Than said. "Shall we discuss the believability of that story as book club members?"

"Than!" Xtelle gasped. "So catty. I approve. Tell us all the sordid details." She hauled the popcorn bag onto her lap again and started munching.

"There are no details," I said.

"I don't think…" Piper bit her bottom lip. "He's not just passing through, Jules. He's here for a reason. I can tell that."

"Because he loves you," Sage said.

That got a laugh out of me. "He doesn't. I promise, he really, really doesn't."

Dusi tipped her head, and I knew from the angle of her mirror sunglasses she was looking over my shoulder. "His body language says he was glad to see you. Glad to have found you, at the very least."

All right. It was time to officially end this conversation. I stood and walked to the tea and snack area.

"Well, that's nice for him," I said. "Xtelle, your lipstick is so…blue. What shade is it?"

"Let's talk about me!" she said. "That's even better."

"Did I mention I have cookies?" I reached into the cupboard for several packs. "Girl Scout cookies."

"Thin mints?" Fawn asked.

"Of course!"

It turned out everyone wanted cookies more than they wanted to gossip about my past. It was easy to change the subject away from Xtelle to when our book club would next meet.

"Festival this weekend," Fawn noted. "Starts Friday."

"I'll be working," Sage said. "You, too, right, Than?"

"Yes. I will be giving tours of the graveyard."

"Wow," Sage said. "I wonder why Bertie picked you for that job."

"Yes," Than said. "One wonders."

Piper snorted and almost choked on her cookie.

"I'll be here working the shop," I said. "So should we meet earlier this week, or later after the Ladle-to-Grave?"

"Still don't think Bertie's going to be able to pull that one off," Fawn said.

"The festival?" Dusi asked. "Why?"

"Wrong time of year," Fawn said. "Bunnies and good luck, that's the spring vibe, not spooky full Worm Moon graveyard tours and seafood chowders. I don't think people are into ghost stories in March."

"Are they not?" Than mused.

"Plus, the rain," Piper said. "I'm not saying it's going to rain, it's just, you know, March."

"Cold, too," Sage said. "And windy. The entire festival is happening at night."

"Are we really accusing Bertie of being wrong?" Dusi asked. "That she's putting on a festival that will fail? Bertie? The Valkyrie who throws a festival every week? The Valkyrie who can out-boss the gods? The Valkyrie who is in fierce festival-running competition with her sister in Drain and hasn't lost yet?"

"Not wrong," I said. "But March is a little unlikely for a Halloween event."

Than just hummed and sipped his tea.

"Boring," Xtelle said. "No one cares about the Ladle-to-Grave. Unless Bertie wants to murder someone and put them in the grave. Now *that* would bring in the crowds."

"Perhaps you should suggest that to Bertie," Than said.

"I did! She told me killing people for profit isn't allowed. Unbelievable. What kind of backwater town is this?"

"The best one," Fawn said.

I laughed.

"I think we should meet after the festival," Sage said.

"Works for me," Piper said. "We'll need to let the rest of the club know."

"All in favor?" I asked.

Everyone said *aye* (except Xtelle who muttered something about reconnaissance) and that was that.

Good-byes were exchanged, and everyone left except Dusi and Piper. I told them they didn't have to, but they insisted on helping me clean up, putting dishes in the dishwasher and the fold-out chairs and tables back where they belonged.

"Do you have the whole day off?" I asked Piper.

"Two days off from the diner, *and* the weekend." She sighed happily. "We're finally back to full staff and I am so glad."

"Nice," I said. "What are you going to do with all that time?"

"Long hot baths and catching up on a couple shows.

Unless someone needs help with her house painting, hint hint."

Dusi took a breath, pausing to think before she spoke.

"I don't need help..."

"Nonsense," I interrupted from the other side of the room. "You know we're happy to pitch in."

"I really don't *need* help," she insisted. "There are only a few rooms waiting for a final coat."

I made a sound.

"Oh, come on," Piper pleaded.

"But," Dusi smiled, "I wouldn't *mind* some help."

"Now you're talking." I gave her a thumbs up. "When should we be over?"

"How about tomorrow?"

"I was hoping you'd say today. But tomorrow works. What time?"

"Eight o'clock?" Dusi asked.

"I'll bring the coffee and tea," I said.

"That means I'm on for muffins," Piper said. "I'll bring some fresh fruit, too, because I can already tell we're going to be hungry."

Hugs were given, and then my two best friends headed out into the drizzly day.

And I was stuck in a quiet shop with nothing to do. So, I called Delaney.

"Police Chief Reed," Delaney answered. "What's up, Jules?"

"Just checking to see if you or your sisters need anything? Tarot reading? Witchery? Help with a crime?"

"We're fine, Auntie. The only thing we're working on right now is prep for the festival."

I wasn't really Delaney's aunt, but when the Reed daughters' mother had passed away, I'd stepped up to be a part of their lives, a part of their support.

I loved those girls and thought of them as my own, even though they were grown now and working as police officers to keep the town (and its secrets) safe.

"Question," I said, "how do you think Ladle-to-Grave is going to go?"

"I think it will be fun. Touring the graveyard, ghost stories, good food, drinks. Hopefully, the photoluminescent jelly fish will be on the beach and we'll have clear skies for seeing the Worm Moon."

"About the weather...."

"Please tell me you haven't messed with the weather. I thought I heard thunder earlier."

"I haven't done anything with the weather."

"No big magic in Ordinary, Auntie."

"No, of course not. But if you wanted me to do a *little* spell..."

"I do not. No magic. It's going to be fine, no matter the weather."

"Yes. Okay. Right. Is there anything else I can do? Any new crime stuff you need tracked down?"

"Not unless Mrs. Yates' penguin is missing."

"No. The spell on it would tell me if it were taken."

"Then we're all good. Thanks for checking in. I know you're busy. Gotta go."

I'd already asked Bertie (several times) if she needed

help with the festival, and had been surprised (several times) that the answer had been no.

Clara's card in my pocket seemed to grow heavier. For a moment—a weak moment—I thought about calling her.

Your life is boring, Juley, because you never take a risk.

Clara's words ran on repeat through my head. But she was wrong. I'd taken plenty of risks in my life.

True, most of them—the big risks—had been years ago.

What exciting thing had I done lately?

Host an emergency book club that ended up not being an emergency?

Even finding the murderer a month ago was mostly me following Dusi around while she solved the crime.

Well, maybe it was time for me to change that. Maybe it was time for me to take a risk I wanted to take.

The idea buzzed through me, and I realized I was humming. Happy. Excited.

Okay, this was good. But what risk should I take?

I climbed the stairs to the second story apartment over the shop.

My home was open and airy, filled with plants, stones, and scarves from my travels. I liked living above my shop, liked living close to the people who came looking for a little bit of magic for themselves.

I crossed the open space to where windows faced west, toward the ocean. My altar was there, and I knelt in front of it.

My fingers drifted across the items: a candle from

bee's wax grown under the new moon, a seashell carved by winter's hands, a feather from the shadow of an owl, moss agate born in the forest's true heart. All was as it should be. From this I would cast magic, a small magic, something even Delaney wouldn't worry about.

So, I gathered the pieces of the spell like a painter sketches a scene, losing myself to the joy of the living world as spirit and magic breathed and danced around me, in my mind, in my soul.

What did I want to attract and manifest? Something exciting. But also something that would allow me to be of service. I wanted to *do* something.

I settled all those thoughts, those yearning emotions into one bell-clear magic:

Call out your need. Call out for assistance. I will find you. I will help you. For if you hear this spell, it tolls for thee.

The spell spooled from my fingers, from my lungs, my words, drifting out over the town, into the sky, into the earth, into the ocean.

"There," I said, still tingling from the magic. "How's that for a risk, Clara?"

Q

MY DREAMS WERE FILLED WITH MEMORIES OF WALKING through a pine forest. I was looking for something, or someone, but with every step the path ahead of me grew foggier.

I paused by a beautiful crystalline stream, and the wind rose, dragging through the branches and leaves above me to make them sing, but somehow not touching the fog.

A voice called, soft as an echo, then growing louder: "Jules Larkwood. Come to me. *Immediately.*"

I jerked and was in my room, the warmth of the dream stripped away.

I shivered and rubbed my arms. The light of the waxing moon slipped behind fast moving clouds, and shadows ballooned and grew thick.

There was no one in my room, but I had heard a voice. Or dreamed a voice.

Had it been a dream? Only one way to find out. I reached out for the tiniest thread of the spell I had cast just a few hours ago.

"Hello?" I said, magic carrying my words where they most needed to be heard. "If you are calling for me, if you need me, I'm listening."

Wind rushed against the windows, and the scent of pine and forest filled the room. I yawned and burrowed deeper under my blankets. Maybe it had been a dream.

"Of course I'm calling for you." The words buzzed along the thread of magic, crackling with static, but loud enough my eyes popped open.

"Yes!" I slapped my hand over my mouth.

"There has been a death," the voice continued.

Be cool, Jules, I thought, *Be cool.*

"Can you tell me where?" I kicked off my blankets. "Can you tell me who? Are you safe?"

I pulled on warm clothes and boots. Silence was my only answer. Whoever had spoken was done.

That was okay. I could tug on the thread and still feel tension there. I should be able to follow the magic string to the speaker and find out what they meant about a death.

I briefly considered calling Delaney but decided against it. It was very early in the morning, and my spell could have gone awry, or the voice could have been some other magical person in town pranking me.

It happened. Lots of supernaturals in one small town meant pranks were a *thing*.

Better not wake Delaney until I gathered more information.

I drove down the deserted main street past quiet buildings and darkened windows, following the thread of magic.

The magic took me to a winding side road, and I instantly knew my destination: the graveyard.

"This isn't creepy," I muttered.

I parked in the gravel area and thought about the mace spray in my glove box. No, my magic would keep me safe if something went sideways.

I got out of the car and wiggled my fingers, pushing magic at the metal gate to unlock it. I stepped through and closed it behind me.

Preparation for the upcoming festival had already started here. Gothic torches taller than me lined the drive and marched out to other paths between the graves. The torches were unlit now, but would cast light during the full moon tour to help guide people through the historic and most interesting areas.

I didn't need light to see the magic that lingered here. Little green and yellow ghost frogs hopped from magical ponds to magical streams flowing beneath trees that no longer existed except in spirit. Ghostly bugs, butterflies, and flowers shifted in a wind I could not feel.

Other ghosts and spirits flickered in and out of sight, and depending on how hard I focused I could see layers of magic over this sacred space that went back centuries.

Just like I could see the thread of my magic leading me onward.

The voice said there had been a death. Maybe that death was part of a crime. A mystery that needed solving. I wanted to keep a cool head, but excitement bubbled through me. I picked up the pace.

Modern, flat gravestones set into the ground tabbed out neatly to either side of me.

But the deeper I went into the older part of the graveyard, the more standing headstones, crosses, angels, and other carved statues marked the lives gone by.

I paused to catch my breath. I was in pretty good shape, for my actual age, but no matter what my body looked like I needed a quick break.

The magic thread continued for another five yards or so, then ended. The voice had to have come from this area, but no one was here.

I turned a slow circle, scanning the graveyard.

Then I saw it. Just ahead and to one side was two mounds of dirt, a lot of it, piled on either side of what had to be a grave.

I slowly walked that way, the dread in my stomach growing stronger.

On top of the dirt was a man's body, whole and intact. He lay on his back, as if he were sleeping, sightless eyes open to the starless sky.

That man was not sleeping. He was very, very dead.

CHAPTER 4

Dead bodies were not my expertise—I'm a witch, not a necromancer. But I loved reading mysteries, watching mysteries, and helping Delaney with local crimes, so I had a fair idea of what a crime scene looked like.

This was a crime scene.

Still, something seemed *off* about this dead body.

First, he was dressed in a three-piece wool suit that looked like it came from another century. Second, his shoes weren't on his feet but were placed neatly in the middle of his chest. Third, his pockets were turned inside out.

And fourth: He was wearing a hat that looked like someone had taxidermized an entire seagull with its wings spread out, feathers sticking up, and plopped it, uh, posterior down, on top of his head.

"What in the worlds?" I turned a circle again. There was no one else out here with me.

Keeping the scene of the crime intact was one of the most important parts of solving a crime but...

...didn't he seem familiar?

I walked a little closer, stopping two yards away from the grave.

He was white, older, heavier set, his face just visible enough to make out the handlebar mustache and goatee.

An electric shock rolled through me. I knew him. Well, *had* known him.

"Professor?" I said quietly, my normally robust voice small and apologetic in the enormity of the moment. "Professor Burgess Carmichael?"

He didn't move (obviously). But the shock of seeing my old magic teacher dead and dug up made me hug my arms across my body. This had to be a joke. A set up. A fake body. Something Bertie was staging for the Ladle-to-Grave.

Professor Carmichael had died years ago. His body should be nothing but a pile of bones, and yet he looked pasty but whole.

A lot of weird things happened in Ordinary, but dead people lying around open graves was not one of them.

I cleared my throat. "I'm sorry you're..." I waved my hand, "...this happened to you. But you don't have to worry. I'm going to call the police and they'll figure it out."

"You will do no such thing."

I screamed and stumbled backward, ghostly frogs scattering from under my feet like hot popcorn. I raised my hands, ready to throw every ounce of magic I could get my fingers on.

He turned his head, nearly dislodging the seabird, and blinked up at me.

"Ms. Larkwood, you are tardy. I called for you nearly an hour ago."

I shook my head and took another step back.

He lowered his hands to the dirt and pushed until he was sitting, moving pretty good for a dead guy. His shoes tumbled off his stomach and landed to one side.

"Assist me." He thrust a dirt-covered hand my way.

"No."

"No?"

"No. You're a…you can't…this is a crime scene."

"Clearly." He awkwardly wiped dirt off his hands, then settled the seabird more firmly on his head. He leaned sideways and twitched his legs.

"What are you doing?"

"Standing." It took a couple tries, but he finally got his legs to do what he wanted and put his feet under him. "There." He shoved upright.

"No. Wait. You can't just walk away from this. It's a *crime scene.*"

"You already stated that. I don't see how it matters."

"You have to lie down. You're part of the crime. You're…you're evidence! Evidence can't stand up and go for a stroll."

He pinned me with a single look that made me feel small and foolish. I hated that feeling.

"Your spell offered assistance to anyone who

answered," he said. "Can you not see that I require assistance?"

"Yes, but…"

"Are you going back on your promise, Ms. Larkwood?"

"You're not even supposed to be alive!"

"That is a moot point." He shook his hand at me again. "Assist me. Now."

Oh, there was no chance I'd let him order me around like that again. I'd left that life decades ago.

I planted my fists on my hips. "You will not take another step out of this graveyard, Mister. Get back in that grave before the chief of police gets here."

"No." He took a step, every inch of him daring me to do something.

"I'm calling the police."

"And how will Daniel Reed help me?"

"Wait. Daniel?"

"The chief of police? He's been here as long as my sister and I have lived in our family home, the Rookery." He pointed vaguely south.

The Rookery was a big old house teetering on the point of a hill jutting out over the ocean. If his sister still lived in Ordinary, she was ancient. And also a hermit. I thought the house had been abandoned years ago.

"Daniel's gone," I said. "Delaney, his daughter, is Chief now."

"Oh." He frowned. "Some time has passed, I suppose. Do you know…is she alive?"

"Delaney?"

"No. My sister, Marlene."

"I don't know."

He made a sad sound and nodded, the bird on his head sliding sideways.

The wind picked up, sieving through shore pines and shuttling clouds across the stars.

Rain spattered around us, and quickly turned into a steady drizzle.

"Great." I pulled up my jacket hood. "So, you'll have to wait…"

"Ms. Larkwood, I have been dead. I woke, cold and now wet, beside my own grave. The police will be of no help to either of us tonight."

He tipped his head down, eyebrows arched, to see if I understood. "Someone raised me from the dead. Only magic will resolve this."

"But why? Why would someone raise *you* from the dead?"

"Are you implying something?"

"And why leave you here in the open? Why bring you back to life and just leave you out here? That's a terrible waste of magic."

"I beg your pardon?"

"Don't scowl at me. It takes a lot of physical effort to dig a grave. Bringing you back to life? That's big magic. And throwing big magic around willy nilly in Ordinary isn't allowed, you know."

"Yes, of course I know that." He wiped rain off his face, streaking his handlebar mustache with mud. "It has been a dreadful night. I need a drink."

I couldn't agree more.

Delaney. I should just call Delaney.

But it was almost four in the morning, and Delaney had been working overtime to prepare for the festival.

It wouldn't make a bit of difference if I called her in the morning. No one wandered around up here, and the police wouldn't be able to investigate the crime scene until daylight. I was more than capable of watching over one grumpy old witch for a few hours.

It started raining harder. Burgess's mustache and seagull looked waterlogged and glum.

"Okay," I said, "fine. Give me a minute."

To make sure no one stumbled upon the crime scene and messed stuff up, I cast a simple spell over the dirt and grave that would repel casual interest and also alert me if anyone came near it.

Burgess grunted in what sounded like grudging approval.

Good thing I didn't care what he thought about my spell casting.

"Car's this way." I started toward it. For a minute, I thought he wasn't going to follow me. Then I heard footsteps and grumbling as he complained about the grass, the mud, the weather, and always just a little bit louder, me.

By the time we reached the car, it was really coming down.

"It's unlocked." I ducked into the driver's seat.

Burgess seemed perplexed at the handle, but after a couple tries, he got the door open. He slowly lowered into the seat, moving at half-speed like he wasn't sure how his knees worked. Then, with great effort, he pulled the door shut.

"Buckle your seat belt," I said.

"No." He pulled the seagull off his head and mopped his face with it. I expected him to smell, well *bad*, but he just smelled like moss and mud.

"Buckle. It's illegal not to wear one."

"Laws are for the living." He shook the gull, flinging water and mud everywhere.

"Stop that. You're alive enough." I pointed at the seatbelt. "Now, Mister."

"Ms. Larkwood." He plopped the bird back onto his head. Backwards. That was a lot of bird butt in my face.

"I am wet, I am cold—a sensation I do not enjoy and have not missed—and I am tired. I will not follow arbitrary mortal rules for mortals. Drive." He made shooing motions. "Now."

"Being dead sure hasn't improved your attitude," I muttered.

"Nor has being alive made you any better at following directions," he huffed.

I resisted the urge to throw him out of the car, and drove. Luckily, he didn't say anything more, too busy staring out into the rain and darkness as the town went by.

I parked behind my shop.

"No funny business, okay? This is it. I live above the shop. Can you walk up stairs?"

"Fool Moon?" Burgess scoffed. "You're living above a shop named Fool Moon?"

"I'm living above *my* shop which I named Fool Moon."

He turned stiffly toward me. In the watery glow from the distant streetlight he looked like death warmed over. Because, well, he was. "Why did you name it that?"

I almost told him. Almost told him my two chosen Tarot cards—the Fool and the Moon—had become my focus, my path.

Back when I'd been a part of his class, the six of us—West, Clara, Burgess, me, and his sister, Marlene, (who had only been in class for one month)—each had a token. On that token were the two major arcana we'd chosen. The tokens were symbols upon which we concentrated our magic.

Maybe it had been an offhand bit of magic to him, something to make us feel like we were special, but that token and magic had grounded me—still grounded me.

The Fool who was willing to step into new adventures, along with the Moon that revealed hidden knowledge, the unknown, and mysteries to be searched, had become core parts of my life. The life I'd built here in Ordinary.

"Stairs," I repeated, not wanting his sour opinion on something important to me. "Can you handle stairs?"

"I'm undead, Ms. Larkwood, not immobile."

"Well then, get mobile."

I ducked out into the rain and hurried to the awning over my door. I unspun the spells of my ward, and unlocked the door then turned on the lights and held the door open for Burgess who shuffled up behind me.

"The stairs are to the right. Living room at top, kitchen on the left, guest room to the right."

He grunted, then laboriously hauled himself up the stairs.

I did a round of the shop, making sure everything was where it should be, making sure everything was secure.

I needed to call Delaney and tell her about the dead man walking I'd put up in my guest room. But calling her felt like I was giving up before I'd even had a chance to do a little investigating on my own.

This crime was technically the opposite of a murder—a revival—which didn't fall under the terms of the bet I'd made with Old Rossi, but still, I wanted to solve who had dug him up, and why they'd done it.

"Just call her," I sighed, knowing I should. "She's the police."

I pulled out my phone. It was almost out of battery—I always forgot to charge it until it was dead—but there should be enough power for a quick chat.

"Chief Reed." Delaney cleared the sleep out of her voice. "What's up, Jules?"

"Are you busy?"

She yawned. "Well, it's...4:15? Just getting some sleep. Pulled an all-nighter."

"Something serious?"

"If you call Mr. Bandy's pigs breaking out and running down the highway serious."

"Pork on the lam."

She snorted. "Slippery, sneaky, smart pork. Took us hours to get them all rounded up." She yawned again. "Sorry. What's up? Is it an emergency?"

"No, not an emergency."

"Okay. Why did you call?"

And just like that, the whole day caught up to me, from West and Clara showing up, to Burgess and his grumpy undeadness. I was suddenly exhausted.

Burgess wasn't going anywhere—my spells would make sure of that. And it wouldn't matter if Delaney investigated the empty grave now or in a couple hours.

I just wanted to get some sleep and figure this all out in the morning.

I chuckled. "You know what, kiddo? It's nothing. I need to talk to you, but it can wait until tomorrow—well, later today. This morning after we both get some sleep."

"Are you sure?" Delaney asked. "If it's important, Auntie..."

"It's not that important. And yes, I'm sure. Get some sleep. I will, too. We'll talk in a couple hours."

Delaney hesitated, and I wondered if she was going to let it go. She had good instincts. She had to know I was giving her the tiniest bit of a brush off. But she also trusted me.

"Okay," she said. "Give me an hour or so of sleep and I'll be over."

"Later if you want. I'll be at the shop. No hurry. Night night."

I ended the call.

There. I'd done my part and let her know...well, let her know she needed to check in. We'd take care of everything else in the morning. We'd get Burgess settled somewhere better than my guest room, and Delaney and her sisters could solve who had raised him from the grave.

Maybe they'd let me do a little magical consultation on the crime, too.

A crash from upstairs startled me. "What are you doing, Burgess?" I shoved my phone in my pocket and tromped up the stairs.

Burgess stood in the center of the living room, in my lovely airy spring space filled with my plants, my comfy furniture, my books.

He was covered in gold glitter. And so was my room.

"What," I asked through my teeth, "are you doing..."

He turned toward me, and I belatedly registered that he was no longer in his three-piece suit but was wearing my long blue skirt and the bulky green sweater I cozied up in during the coldest weather.

"...wearing my clothes?" I demanded.

He drew himself up and sniffed. "I didn't assume you had a spare suit that would fit me. This will have to do."

He picked at the sleeve and shed glitter like a unicorn in a high wind.

"Why are you covered in glitter? Did you get into my craft chest?"

"I thought it was a bottle of cologne."

"In my craft chest?"

"In the guest room closet. Where I was forced to find new clothing. I'm undead, Ms. Larkwood, I haven't lost my mind."

Arguable, I thought.

"Shower. You need to get in the shower. You have glitter *everywhere.*"

"I don't want…"

"Shower. That way. Now."

"You can't just—"

"Oh, yes, I can. And don't touch anything. I'll be picking up glitter for months."

He said something rude under his breath, then shambled down the hall to the guest bedroom and attached bath. I heard the bathroom door open, the water turn on, and the bathroom door slam shut.

Why? I silently mouthed to the heavens.

Then I took a deep breath. Until I knew that dead guy was safely sleeping—if he even slept—there was no chance I'd get any sleep either .

So, I pulled the vacuum out of the closet and got to work on the glitter.

CHAPTER 5

I staggered out of bed and into the shower, hopeful that hot water and a stiff cup of tea would revive me. Sleep? Maybe two hours.

But Delaney would be here soon to take care of Burgess, so two hours would have to do.

I was trying to convince myself to be happy about her taking over the case. It wasn't much of a case, anyway—not something dangerous and exciting like a murder.

Well, raising the dead wasn't a small thing. Someone had to have used big magic to pull off that kind of spell in Ordinary.

Maybe I'd ask him a few more questions before Delaney got here just to, you know, gather some information for her.

I turned off the water, toweled, and put on leggings, skirt, and a flowing top. I added bracelets and necklaces and sprayed on a little product to scrunch up my hair so it would dry in waves.

"Nice," I said to the thirty-year-old looking me in the mirror. For a moment, just the flash of a thought, I wondered what I would look like if I removed my youth spell or if I modified it so I looked older, like West.

How would my fifties look on me? How would my sixties?

No. No time for that, no time for him. I had enough problems.

Maybe Burgess could answer a few questions over breakfast.

I found him in the kitchen standing in front of the open refrigerator.

"Finally," he said. "I've been waiting for hours."

His skin looked even worse in the morning light. It was pale and also greenish, shadows around his eyes, temples, and cheeks bruised brown and yellow. He looked like a potato that had been at the bottom of the barrel so long it was beginning to rot.

Or maybe he looked like he'd been dead and dug up in the middle of the night.

His hair was still a mess, his mustache a bit droopy. He'd put on a second sweater from my guest closet. This one was black.

"Hours?" I asked. "Have you been standing there all night?"

"How would I know?" He bent to retrieve something off a shelf. "Time means nothing to me."

He turned, a block of cheese in one hand. He pulled down the plastic that kept it fresh and took a huge bite.

Ew.

"That isn't—what are you doing?"

"Eating," he said through a mouth of cheese. His face screwed up as he tried to swallow. "Dreadful," he squeaked, spitting the cheese into his hand.

He considered the chewed cheese in one hand, the block in the other and took another bite of the block.

"Burgess!"

He glared at me.

"Professor Carmichael." I pointed at the table. "Stop chewing on my cheese, stop rummaging through my guest closet, and sit down."

He chomped off another chunk of cheese and chewed out of pure spite, then seated himself and spit the entire mess onto the table.

"Oh, for Pete's—" I snatched the cheese out of his hand and tossed a towel at him. "Clean up your mess. Please."

He narrowed his eyes, then glared at the cheese as if it were at fault. He woodenly scooped the mess into the towel.

"Terrible cheese," he muttered. "No taste at all."

I took a settling breath and tried to remember that being undead was new to him. I didn't think anyone would handle the reality of it gracefully. So what if he spit a little dairy product on my table? It was easy enough to clean.

I filled the tea kettle and gathered two cups.

"It's morning," I said evenly. "I've called Delaney Reed. She'll be here to help soon." I cut oranges into wedges, filling the room with the bright, sweet citrus scent. I put the fruit in a bowl.

"She's very good at her job. I think she can find out who dug you up and who revived you and why. She'll put everything to right."

"Everything?" he mused, "I don't see how she could."

"Well, she's your best bet. You'll need to tell her everything you remember."

"I don't remember anything."

I very much doubted that. I put a tea bag in each cup, then poured the water. Even if he couldn't eat, the scent of fruit and tea were soothing.

"Do you remember waking up by the grave?" I set his tea in front of him and took the oranges and my tea and sat opposite him.

"I—" He frowned. "The sky. I saw clouds. I was stretched out on the ground. On the *dirt*. So undignified."

"Did you pull yourself out of the grave?" The oranges were as sweet as they smelled. Delicious.

He shook his head.

"Do you remember how you got out of the grave?"

He shook his head again.

Someone must have helped him. It was a detail Delaney would pick up on, I was sure. "Before you died, did you set up a spell to bring yourself back from the dead?"

"I beg your pardon? Use dark magics?" His face looked like a dead guy who had chomped through a crate of lemons. Or half a block of cheese. "Of course I *know* dark magic, but using it has always been beneath me."

Yeah, he had always gone on about what kind of magic was the right kind of magic any of us should use. He often repeated that only the best and strongest witches could handle dark magic. And he'd just as often reminded me that I was neither best nor strong.

"Do you know if there's a time limit on you being... um...like this?"

"Are you asking me if I'll go rotten like an old onion?"

"No." *Yes.*

He crossed his arms. "I do not know. When the full moon comes around, we'll find out."

Chills rolled down my arms. "Full moon?"

"When the moon—the celestial body in the sky—is full. That means it's big and round to the visible eye."

"I know what a full moon is. What happens to *you* at a full moon?"

He peered down into his teacup. "Is this green tea? Deplorable stuff. Gives me gas."

"Burgess, what happens to you at the full moon?"

His cloudy gaze ticked up then cut to the side. "We'll find out, I suppose."

So, he didn't want to tell me what he suspected, or maybe he really didn't know what would happen, and couldn't admit his ignorance.

I finished off the last orange wedge and glanced at the clock over his shoulder. The shop needed to be open in three minutes.

"Can you tell me one thing? How did you die?"

He lifted his chin and those beady eyes went hard with a dark intensity. "I was murdered."

A little thrill ran through me. Hadn't I just been asking for something exciting to happen? It didn't have to be murder, but I mean, murder was a plus. (I knew how that sounded, I wasn't a ghoul.) And here he was, telling me he'd been the victim of a crime.

It was just what I'd been hoping for!

Which made me suspicious. When did a murder happen just because you wanted it to?

"Did they find out who killed you?"

That sour face returned. "How would I know? I was dead."

"Then how do you know you were murdered?"

"Because I was sitting in my study, in the house that belongs to my sister and me…"

"You lived with your sister?"

"Hardly. We didn't get along well enough to live in the same town much less the same house. We had an agreement. I would live in the Rookery during half the year, and she would live there the other half of the year. I preferred winters, of course."

Of course you did, I thought. *Miserable weather suits you.*

"Go on. You were in your study…"

His eyes glazed. "I was reading. The door opened swiftly. There were footsteps. I turned and light blinded me."

He stopped, his mouth ajar, like maybe accessing those memories had short-circuited him for good. I waited to see if he'd start back up.

"Did you cast magic?"

"Of course not. I demanded they tell me who they were, and then…"

Eyes drifted, mouth hung. I didn't wait around this time.

"Then they killed you?"

He closed his mouth and nodded. "Then they killed me. An unsatisfying exit from the world. I hadn't even finished the book. Now I'll never know how it ended."

"Did the killer use magic? Or shoot you? Or strangle you or…*how* did you die?"

"Magic. It had to be. I have no obvious marks on my body, no memory of pain. I was alive, *reading*, and then I was not."

There weren't that many supernaturals or normals who could use killing magic in Ordinary. Delaney wouldn't allow it. Or, I suppose back then, her father Daniel wouldn't allow it.

His killer had to have been caught. That much magic wouldn't have escaped the notice of the Reed family. Besides them finding a dead body, the magic would have left a mark, a hint, a clue that it had been used.

But that magical mark faded over time, so tracing it now would be a dead end.

I knew I wasn't going to solve this mystery, and it was entirely possible his killer (if he wasn't just making this up to be dramatic) had already been caught.

Still, it wouldn't hurt to get as much information as I could.

"How long ago was this?"

"What year is it now?"

I told him and he did some not-very-quick math. "Forty years ago," he said.

Oh, yeah. The magic mark was long gone.

"But my murderer is still here. In this town." He pushed up, one hand on the table to correct his wobble.

"You can't know that. You've been dead, remember?" I gathered dishes and put the orange rinds in the compost pail.

"Being dead has nothing to do with it. I know my murderer is in town."

"How?" I washed my hands and dried them on the flowered towel hanging off the oven door. I was going to be late opening the shop.

"It's Magic 101, Ms. Larkwood," he said with enough attitude, I was almost sorry I'd asked.

"To raise a witch from the dead," he went on, "one must be the person who killed the witch in the first place. Magic 101. Look it up."

That...that wasn't a rule I'd ever heard of before.

But if he was right, there was a killer loose in my town.

CHAPTER 6

Burgess refused to answer any more of my questions. Instead, he wandered over to rummage through my kitchen cupboards.

"Burgess? Are you listening? I'm going downstairs to open the shop."

"Go away."

"Fine, be that way," I said. "Just stay out of trouble—and out of my glitter—until Delaney gets here."

He opened my spice drawer and pawed through it, muttering about my organizational skills.

I shook my head and tromped downstairs.

The back room was still tidy from the emergency book club meeting.

Had it only been yesterday? Dealing with the undead guy all night had really messed with my sense of time.

I sent magic ahead of me to flip on the lights and music, then I turned the sign to OPEN and unlocked the door.

It wasn't like anyone was waiting at my doorstep. It was Tuesday, and foggy enough, everything dripped. I spotted Marty strolling across the street, coffee mug in one hand.

He waved and I held the door open for him.

"Morning, Auntie." His voice was low and carried some of the humor and magic he'd inherited from his parents. He had good eyes, my nephew, soft and brown and almost glowing. He got them from his mother, who was a Cheruf—a creature of crystal and magma.

He wore a black hoodie, jeans, and a beanie with an O surrounding the letters "R-D-I-N-A-R-Y".

He appeared to be in his early forties, and had his father's—my wayward brother's—dashing good looks. He fortunately had his mother's brains and empathy. It was no wonder Dusi had been smitten with him from the first moment she saw him.

I just wished the two of them would stop dancing around each other and go on a date. They had a chance for happiness right in front of them. I didn't know what they were waiting for.

"Life is short, you know," I said.

His eyebrows rose. "Where's that coming from?"

"I saw Dusi yesterday…"

He laughed, and it was a good, deep chuckle. "This is me gently pushing your nose out of my business. Thank you, Auntie."

"All right. Well, Delaney's going to be by soon."

"For police stuff, or to shop?" He moved around the counter to start setting up the till.

"To talk. About things. The Ladle-to-Grave festival, and etcetera."

He made a noncommittal sound. "Seems like Bertie has this one running pretty smoothly."

"I still need to talk to Delaney."

"If you're asking me to handle the shop while she's here, it's not a problem. Oh, before I forget, the board gamers need some extra time this week. Are you okay with us being here? I'll handle set up and clean up."

"Sage already asked. It's fine with me. This game thing is really getting popular, isn't it?"

"It is." His excitement was contagious. "We're keeping our group small, but I think I could fill a shop this size with gamers every night. Add a little coffee and food service, and, yeah, people would hang."

"A game café?"

"Mainly board games, but it could be more. A place to listen to music, meet with friends, read. I'd set up a lending library of some kind."

"You'd need a lot of foot traffic to keep it going."

"Already ahead of you. I'd put on themed events to go alongside Bertie's festivals. Salem has Ticket to Play and it's fantastic. Portland has Mox Boarding House, which is also fantastic. It could work in a small town like ours."

"I haven't seen you excited about work in a long time, nephew. Are you serious about this?"

"If the right space opened up, yes. I might give it a go."

A thump rattled the ceiling and something rolled from one end of the room to the other.

Marty glanced up. "Is someone up there? Want me to check it out?"

"No, it's fine. I'll go."

"Are you sure?" Curiosity animated his face, and his eyes practically sparkled.

"It's fine. I have a…visitor."

"A *visitor*. Good for you, Auntie." He winked.

"Not like—not that kind of—never mind. You finish opening. I'll be right back."

I took the stairs to my living room.

Chaos. Pillows on the floor, couch cushions thrown about, books pulled off the shelves and stacked in teetering piles—one of which had fallen over—probably the thump. My Magic Eight Ball collection now lined one wall like a row of prognosticating bowling balls waiting for the next frame.

"Burgess Carmichael. You are a menace." I clenched my fists and started toward the sound of rustling coming from the guest room. "Burgess. This is unacceptable."

The rustling became more furious.

I wanted to barge in there, but I didn't relish the idea of catching him undressed.

So, I knocked. Firmly.

"I'm coming in."

"Don't you dare!"

Too late. I opened the door and stepped in.

I had put time and effort into making the guest room cozy. I'd painted the walls the softest rose and decorated with little items from my travels—framed maps and photos, soft pillows, and a gloriously comfy easy chair.

Burgess had gone through the room like a drunken wrecking ball.

The dresser drawers (empty) all hung open. The blankets were tangled on the ground in piles and the bed had been pulled away from the wall.

He'd sorted all the artwork and travel mementoes into heaps. On those heaps he'd used random notebook paper to write TRIVIAL and HORRID.

Burgess himself stood half in, half out of the closet like he'd just been caught with his hand in the cookie jar.

The seagull hat was perched haphazardly on his head, his hair sticking straight out from under it like a gray nest. His mustache was combed and twisted up into two jaunty points.

He wore my winter tights (red with little candy canes), another of my skirts (bright purple), and the same baggy cardigan he'd had on this morning.

Every piece of clothing I'd stored in the closet was mounded at his feet. He clutched a bottle of—I wanted to say body spray—I'd forgotten I'd had in one hand, and a lacy umbrella in the other.

"How dare you," he puffed, swinging the umbrella in front of him like he was challenging me to a duel.

"What are you doing in my...everything?"

"Your everything? I'm a guest here. This is a guest room. Therefore, it's *my* everything."

"That isn't...you can't just..." I shut my mouth before I started yelling. "You will pick this up and put it back where it was, Mister. Immediately."

He raised his chin. "I am not a child, Ms. Larkwood. And though I am not alive like you, I am still human."

Heat prickled down my face and neck. Anger, sure, but also a tiny bit of shame. I didn't like him, I'd never liked him, but I never wanted anyone thinking I didn't see them as human.

"Then be human," I said with less heat. "Stop ransacking my house. And put everything back where it was, the way it was. Please."

"Fine," he said.

"Fine," I said.

He didn't move, I didn't move. "I'll be downstairs."

"Good."

"I'm coming back up here as soon as Delaney shows up."

"Yes, yes. The police. I know."

"You'll put everything back where you found it. All of it."

He glared at me and made jabbing motions with the umbrella.

"For the love of the goddess," I grumbled. I left him to it, and spent a few moments straightening up the worst of the living room mess before hurrying back downstairs.

A handful of tourists were picking up and putting down rune stones, yoga cat statues, crystals, and other bits and bobs. A woman with pink hair was taking advantage of the Tarot corner. She sat cross-legged on the green velvet bench, several boxes of Tarot at her side as she thumbed through the Light Seer's deck.

"Good choice," I told her. "That's one of my favorites."

She looked up and smiled. "It's gorgeous."

"And such good energy."

She nodded and went back to looking through the cards.

Marty had lit a stick of sandalwood incense and switched the music to something soft that had a nice beat.

It was cloudy and breezy outside, making my shop a cozy little nest in the middle of a chilly March day.

I fell into the routine of tidying the merchandise, answering customer questions, and otherwise chatting with Marty.

I was almost surprised three hours had passed by the time Delaney walked in.

She was taller than me, and built athletically, whereas folks would describe me as voluptuous. Her hair was brown and she had the blue eyes that ran in the Reed family. Instead of her uniform, she wore a flannel jacket, jeans, and boots.

"Hey, Jules," she said. "Hi, Marty."

"Morning." Marty glanced at the clock to make sure it was still morning. "Coffee?"

She shook her head and smiled ruefully. "Any more, I'll start vibrating. So, what's up Jules?"

"Come on back."

I led her to the storage and sitting room. "Tea?" I offered.

She made herself comfortable. "I'm good," she said

around a yawn. "Sorry I'm late. I had to handle a few things this morning. Did you know that a fence six inches on the wrong side of a property line is an emergency that will take two hours to settle?"

"Is this a new fence?"

"Nope. Been there for decades. The homeowner is just annoyed he hasn't been invited to the neighbor's new hot tub."

"Totally needed to get the police involved," I said, and she chuckled.

"It is my duty to serve. So what did you need to talk about?"

I finished making a cup of masala chai. Strong. I was going to need it. "I know you might be angry with me, but I promise everything is in control."

She straightened, her eyebrows lifting. "Not the best way to convince me everything is in control. What happened? Are you okay?"

"I'm good. But I was bored…"

She groaned and rubbed a hand over her face. "What did you do?"

"I wanted to help. You know I only want to help. So, I cast a small spell."

"Auntie."

"Small, Delaney. It was just a little…I suppose it was a beacon. A promise that if someone needed help, they could reach out to me. Don't give me that look. It's not against the rules to use a little magic to help people in this town."

"I know the rules," she said. "What happened?"

I took a sip of tea and sat opposite her.

"Someone answered the spell. He needed help. I followed the magic to find him."

"When was this?"

"Early morning. Just after three o'clock."

"Jules. You didn't call me until almost four."

"I didn't call you because as far as I knew it could have been someone who had a flat tire."

"That's something you should still call me about."

"I'd call Frigg's Rigs about a flat tire. You don't have to deal with every little problem in this town, you know."

"That is literally my job. Was it a flat?"

"It was not. It was a, uh, just a dead man."

"What?"

"But he wasn't dead! He was dug up. By his grave. And not dead, I repeat. I mentioned not dead? That's good, the not-dead part. I knew him a long time ago—he's always been a bit of a jerk—and I was going to call you.

"Oh! I did, I called you. But it was raining, and you'd been out chasing pigs, and he wanted a shower, and I set a spell around the grave so it wouldn't be disturbed. That means the crime scene is still intact. That's good, too.

"And well, here we are now. It's only been a few hours, so no harm done."

She took a deep breath. "Undead? Like a zombie? That is important, Jules. He was dug up? In the grave-yard? You should have told me."

"I was tired. You were tired."

"That doesn't matter. A dead man dug up and zombified is big. That's absolutely a problem for me to solve no matter how tired I was. That is not a problem for you to solve."

"I wasn't solving it. I was just putting it on hold until you came here to fix it."

She stood and crossed her arms over her chest. "Where is he?"

"Upstairs."

"You brought him here?" She shook her head and started up the stairs.

I followed her, breathing past the tight feeling in my chest. I had wanted to help. And there hadn't been any harm in me letting us both get some sleep—other than the mess he'd made in my living room and guest room.

I supposed my thirst for adventure had made me a little more reckless than I should have been, but regardless of what Burgess thinks, I am a powerful witch. I have magic to keep me safe.

At the top of the stairs her body went tense. She threw her arm out to one side to keep me from going any further. "Your house."

"He tore it apart this morning, I know. He's probably in the guest room."

Delaney dropped her arm and stepped into the space.

Good news? It wasn't any worse than it had been earlier, so maybe he'd actually spent his time cleaning up the guest room.

"Burgess?" I called. "Delaney Reed is here to help you now."

"You said you knew him?"

I walked down the hall to the guest room. "Years ago. He taught magic."

"Is Burgess his full name?"

"Burgess Carmichael."

She frowned.

I knocked on the door. No answer. "We're coming in now."

The room was still in disarray. But Burgess was not there.

I pointed back toward the main room. "Maybe he's in the kitchen. Burgess?"

"Mr. Carmichael?" Delaney called out in what I thought of as her friendly authority voice. "I'm Chief Reed and I'm here to help you. Can we talk?"

"He's here," I said glancing in the main room. "He was right here." I headed to my bedroom and Delaney strode to the kitchen.

My bedroom, at least, had been untouched. But he was nowhere to be seen.

"Anything?" I asked as I joined her in the kitchen.

"This." Delaney handed me a piece of paper.

It was in Burgess's cramped handwriting, but I didn't register the words. Because there was a bottle on my table. An empty bottle. I'd seen that bottle in his hands. I'd thought it was body spray.

It wasn't body spray. It was a very old potion I'd mixed up on a lark.

An invisibility spell.

CHAPTER 7

"Wait a minute," Piper said, the roller in her hand loaded with...I wanted to say Space Pigeon blue. "You went to the graveyard at three in the morning. By yourself?"

I dipped my brush into paint called Greenish (lazy naming if you asked me) and carefully painted the edge of the wall.

Over the last couple weeks Dusi's house had been transformed from a basic beige rental, into a lovely, colorful home that made me feel like I'd stepped into a sunlit meadow full of plants and flowers.

"Someone was calling for my help. Of course I went to help them."

"You should have called us." Dusi applied painter's tape to the floor molding. She had a pot of Vanilla Onion ready to go.

Tufa, the little golem otter she'd made, was running across the floor, pulling a wad of tarp after him. He was trying to shove the whole thing into the empty fireplace, where he'd already accumulated several stir sticks, a pillow, and an assortment of scarves.

"It was the middle of the night," I said.

"As if that matters," Dusi said.

"You know what?" Piper glanced over at me. "I predict that the next time you hear an undead voice calling you out to the graveyard *in the middle of the night,* you are going to call us, aren't you?"

"That sounds more like an order than a prediction." I laughed.

"Good ears," she said. "Now tell us about the dead guy."

"He was my teacher—well, he taught Clara, West, Marlene, and me. He was, he *is,* a judgmental, petty person, and an all-around sourpuss. But seeing him lying there by his grave with that dead seagull on his head...I don't know. He needed help, so I helped him."

"He told you his killer raised him from the dead?" Dusi asked.

"Not quite. He said the only person who could raise a witch from the dead was the person who had killed them. But that's not a rule of magic I've ever heard before."

"Did you tell Delaney there might be a murderer in town?"

"I did. I told her a lot of things. For almost two hours. Straight." I painted the next spot a little aggressively. "She's very good at her job."

"Can you track him down with magic?" Piper asked.

"Not while he's invisible, no. When I made that potion, I was trying to push the limits on just how invisible a spell might make someone. Turns out it's so invisible, even magic can't find him."

"Delaney will figure it out," Dusi said, but I could hear her doubt.

"There are a lot of supernaturals in town who could help find him," Piper added. "Right?"

"I don't think so. I really brewed up a doozy."

"Well, then Delaney is going to have her work cut out for her."

"What I don't understand," Dusi said, "is why someone would go through all the effort to raise him from the dead and then leave him by the grave."

"Maybe he opened his mouth and they got a sample of his personality," I muttered.

Piper snickered. "Also, if it was grave robbing, and not just dead-raising, then maybe someone was there to steal something."

I stopped, mind spinning. I'd been so caught up in the problem of him being alive that I hadn't really taken the time to think that something might have been buried with him.

Something someone—maybe the killer—wanted.

"Is that a random thought, or are you *seeing* something?"

Piper paused. She had a pink kerchief over her hair, and the smudge of blue on her cheek made her wide gray eyes look like storm water.

"It's not a seeing, not a seer thing. Plus, I don't *see* the only future, exactly, but sort of a general, probable future."

"So, the grave robbing is just a guess?" I asked.

"Mostly? I think there has to be a reason he was dug up, a *thing* the grave robber wanted."

Dusi shook her head. "But if they just wanted to rob the grave, why bring him back to life?"

"Maybe that was an accident?" Piper said. "Can someone be re-alived accidentally?"

I shrugged. "Magic is different in Ordinary. Different than out there where the rules of Ordinary don't constrain and sometimes change it. It *could* be possible he was accidentally brought back to life. But it's not likely."

"Which means we're looking for a necromancer," Dusi said. "Or a god."

"Or a witch who dabbles in that kind of magic," I said.

"Or any other supernatural in town who can bring people back from the dead," Piper added.

"And that's why it's Delaney's job to deal with it." I straightened up and assessed my handiwork.

"Of course it is," Dusi said.

"Very practical," Piper said.

We painted for a little longer. Tufa tried to steal Dusi's paint can lid, but she swiped it from him just in time. He dodged around her and chomped on a roll of paper towels, running with them as fast as he could back to his nest.

Dusi laughed. "Bring those back, you scamp. I need them for clean up."

Tufa just chittered and stuffed the towels into his nest.

"Delaney's very good at her job," I said.

Dusi made a sound of agreement. Piper nodded.

She didn't need my help solving the case. I knew that.

But I really wanted to solve it. I was a part of it, or at least Burgess was a person from my past, and that made me feel like I was a part of the case.

Plus, I'd bet Rossi I would solve the next murder in town and Burgess had said he'd been murdered. It might be an old murder, but I didn't know if the killer had been caught.

"We totally have to figure out who the murderer is!" Piper blurted.

"Oh, my stars, yes!" I said.

"Finally," Dusi agreed.

I laughed. "Thank you both! It is driving me up the wall to not solve this. Burgess said his killer had to be in town, so I know Delaney's looking for him. I did promise her I wouldn't get in the way of her investigation."

"You didn't get in the way of the last investigation when I was accused of murder," Dusi said.

"Which we solved," Piper added. "Before Delaney."

"That could have been beginner's luck," I said, "but there's only one way to find out—solve another crime. Burgess didn't remember anything about the person who killed him. Just that he was interrupted while reading in his house."

"So where do we start?" Piper asked. "Should we figure out what valuable thing was taken from his grave? Would that lead us to the killer?"

"Or should we track down the person who might already know what valuables he had?" Dusi asked.

"Burgess?" Piper asked.

Dusi nodded and one of the snakes who was curled up in a cute little bun lifted its head and wiggled, agreeing with her. "Can you find the invisible man without magic?"

"Maybe?" I wrapped my brush in a plastic bag so I could put it in the fridge or freezer until it was time to paint with it again. "I know where I'd start looking, anyway."

They both watched me expectantly.

"If you were looking for him..." Piper prompted.

"If I were looking for him, I'd start where he lived when he was here. The Rookery."

They both frowned.

"It's that old house up on the cliff."

"The spooky abandoned one?" Piper asked.

"I haven't thought about that place in decades," Dusi said.

"None of us have, really, with the trees grown up around it," I said. "I don't even know if his sister still lives there. He said they used it like a time share."

"Are they immortal?" Dusi asked.

Which, yeah, fair question. "Not exactly, but they were both powerful witches and that gave them a few extra decades."

"Like you," Piper said.

"Like me."

"So, when are we going to go see if she lives there?" Piper asked.

"Delaney knows all this. Should we let her question her first?"

Piper blinked and threw a look Dusi's way.

"Jules," Dusi said gently. "You sent out the spell searching for people who needed your help. He needed your help. He still needs your help. Someone raised him from the dead and that person may be a killer who may be in this town. Delaney's doing her part, but you still need to do yours."

"True. Even if Delaney has already talked to her—if Marlene is even there—she might tell me something else. Something that could help with the case."

"So?" Piper asked.

"So?"

"So, when are we going to talk to his sister?"

"How about now?" I asked.

"Yay!" Piper said.

"Good choice." Dusi set her brush down and picked up a scarf to cover the snakes. "Come here, Tufa. It's time for an adventure."

Q

THE ROOKERY WAS A MULTI-STORY BUILDING BUILT STAGGERED against the cliff, its many windows facing west, the cedar-shake roof peaked with multiple chimneys. I wanted to say the paint was once yellow, but it had faded to the color of the sand several stories below it.

The road up to the place was narrow and rutted, the asphalt cracked, so I was driving as slowly as I could. Dusi, Piper, and a napping Tufa were along for the ride.

The day had flirted with sun breaks, but had given up and was now a steady drizzle.

I couldn't remember how long it had been since I'd wandered up here on the south end of town. Years. Maybe decades.

I put the car in park in front of the building and turned off the engine.

"This isn't..." Piper pressed her lips together and gave a little shake of her head.

"What?"

"You know I see...things."

"It's a wonderful gift."

She wrinkled her nose, then laughed. "Not always so wonderful. But I don't know." She waved at the house. "I don't know how helpful this is going to be."

"Dangerous?" Dusi tucked a lap throw over Tufa, who was snuggled in that ridiculous kangaroo purse I'd given her. He had refused to give up the roll of paper towels, clutching it like a baby-otter sized body pillow.

"I don't think so? But there are some *things* that might be? That doesn't make sense, does it? I'm usually clearer on the future than this."

"That's okay," I said. "If you want to stay out here…"

"No!"

I laughed and patted her knee. "Well, then, let's go."

I got out of the car, Piper and Dusi right on my heels.

We strolled up to the porch with its own peaked roof that had slumped on one corner. The gutter was detached and leaking. The house had once been a gloriously gaudy old thing—the closest to a mansion Ordinary had ever had. But time and neglect had left their mark.

It still had good bones—it had weathered all the storms over the years and was still standing—but it could certainly use some tender loving repair.

I rang the bell. I didn't even know if anyone lived here. Didn't know if Marlene was still alive. I rang the bell a couple more times.

I really should have done some asking around before just driving out here and expecting—

—the door swung open.

"Are you here to buy the house?" Marlene (it had to be Marlene) was short and wide, swathed in layer after layer of autumn-colored knitted wear. I put her at a spry ninety-seven, even though her hair was a shiny black bob that I was pretty sure had to be a wig.

Her eyes (and glare) looked so much like Burgess, that all my defenses automatically kicked in.

"We're not here to buy the house."

Shoot, I thought. *Why hadn't I said yes and asked for a tour?*

"Then get off my property."

"We would like to come in and talk to you," I said, taking a step forward. "It's about your brother."

"He's dead."

"We want to talk about that. And where you were last night."

She didn't react, didn't move. Since I'd stepped forward, we were uncomfortably close. She smelled strongly of garlic and cinnamon.

I looked down at her, she glared up at me, and then, faster than I'd expect for a bird her age, she scuttled backward deeper into the house.

"Shut the door," she commanded. "You're letting in the damp. This house is historical. People should appreciate how historical it is."

I glanced back at Piper, who rolled her eyes. Dusi made a shooing motion and shut the door behind us.

The interior was lit well enough to show off the brown-plastered walls, brown faded wallpaper, and brown hardwood floors covered in layers of rugs.

The main theme of decoration against all that brown was: birds.

They were everywhere. Pictures and collectibles and pillows, yes. But the room was also cluttered with real birds—taxidermized and perched on top of shelves, tables, nested along the walls, and even suspended from the ceiling.

Most were beach birds, but there were a few rarer feathered fellows, a robin, a crow, a tiny finch, flying their corpse-ified colors.

"Burgess, you said? I knew it would come to this,"

Marlene croaked as she settled herself on a couch that had once been covered in...I wanted to say red velvet... and pulled four blankets over her lap before adjusting the pillows behind her.

"That man was nothing but trouble. Ask me how many times I had to remind him to pay his half of the property taxes. Every year. Useless!" she yelled at the ceiling.

A thump, like a door slamming on the upper floor rang through the house.

"Wind," she said grumpily. "These old walls are sieves. Historical buildings are drafty as old Billy heck, but the draft makes them authentic."

"Um," I said, "yes. It's a lovely home. Can you tell me where you were last night?"

"I was here last night. I am *always* here in the evenings and the mornings and the afternoons. I don't go *out*. Filthy old world. Sit down. All of you are too tall. Are you trying to make my neck sore?"

Piper made a sound that was half laughter, and Dusi looked like she might want to lower her sunglasses so she and Marlene could have a little stare down. (It wouldn't end well for Marlene.)

Then Piper walked over and carefully lowered herself to the couch opposite Marlene. She patted the couch.

"Come sit down, Jules," she said, brightly. "Think of her neck."

"The neck." I nodded gravely. "Of course." I gingerly settled next to her. The old couch didn't so much as creak. I figured it was made when builders used cast iron frames and battleship rivets.

Dusi crossed her arms and remained standing behind us.

"So," I said, trying to ease into this. "I wanted to ask you a few—"

"I gave up magic," she interrupted. "Too much trouble. He thought he was the only one who could cook up a good spell, but I've proved that egotistical nonsense wrong. I'm better than him. I've always been better than him. But I'm done with it! You're welcome."

"Um, yes. Okay, no magic. Interesting. What I was going to ask—"

"No, we didn't get along. I never liked him, and he never liked me. He was bossy, interrupted constantly, and was a *bully*!" She yelled that last bit. "There. I said it."

Another bang clattered from above us. It sounded like something was chasing a ball across the ceiling.

"Stupid historical house." She pulled a stuffed bird with a huge bill into her lap and aggressively petted its head.

"So historical," I said. "So about last night…"

"Also, he never kept his sticky fingers to himself. He took things, you know. *My* things. My bone-cleaning crock pot, my chinchilla dust. He never respected my boundaries."

"Chinchilla dust?" I said.

"It's for the feathers. You don't want dirty, soggy-looking feathers, do you?"

"No one would want that," Piper said. "Unless they were historical?"

"They are not."

"I heard you both owned the house," I tried. "You stayed the summers here on a time share schedule when he was alive?"

"Winter. He always wanted winter. That's what killed him, you know."

"The season?"

She stopped petting the...maybe pelican?...and squeezed it so hard, its head tilted so that it was staring at me, wide-eyed with panic.

"Magic. Winter," she said. "What do you think I mean? Who are you again? Do I know you?"

"Jules Larkwood. We were both students in one of Burgess's classes years ago. The, uh, Star Wards Arcana."

"That thing where we used two Tarot cards to focus our magic and *blah, blah, blah,* take over the world, immortality, *blah.*"

World? Piper mouthed.

"There were no plans to take over the world." I turned to Piper. "You know I wouldn't be a part of that."

"Of course not."

"No plans?" Marlene snorted. "My body might be petrifying, but my memory's clear as a...what are those clear things that make that sound? A jell! Clear as a jell.

"Burgess was *absolutely* trying to take over the world. Never stopped talking about it. He used all of us and our powers to try to do it, too, the sticky-fingered twit."

Somewhere in the back of my mind bits of things that never added up clicked into place.

He *had* pitted us against each other, and then insisted we give him our tokens until we made peace. And while the tokens weren't in themselves valuable—just silver charms with symbols of Tarot—they *were* personal, and they did carry our magic. Magic I now wondered if he'd tried to tap into and use.

I had hated giving him my token, and I knew Clara and West felt the same.

"You said winter killed him?" Piper said. "That sounds terrible. Can you give more details on that?"

"Do you not know that people die?" She shifted to glare at me. "Does she not understand people die?"

"Oh, no, she does," Dusi said from behind us. "We just want to know if someone murdered him."

Marlene went still. "Murder? Are you accusing me of murdering my lying, thieving, self-centered jerk of a brother whom I've never liked?"

This time the sound from above was glass shattering. Maybe a vase falling off a table.

"Wind," Marlene, Piper, Dusi, and I all said at the same time. We exchanged a look (well, not Dusi, not directly) and even Marlene gave us a brief smile. It was a nice moment but it passed quickly.

"Do you know if he was murdered?" I asked. "I'm not saying you murdered him. I'm just wondering how he died."

She hopped down from the couch and brandished the pelican at me. "If anyone deserved to murder him, it was me!" For how tiny she was, she sure had a set of lungs on her. "Get out of my house, Jules Larkwood, if that really is your name. Out!"

She stabbed the pelican in my general direction.

"Out!"

I stood, Piper stood. Dusi made a sound like she'd been tired of that kind of behavior for centuries.

"Could I...uh...would you mind if I used your bathroom?" I asked. It was an old ploy to give me some time to snoop around her house.

"Of course I mind. No bathroom. Out! Out, out!" She really got going with the bird, and it was clear she had fencing training in her past.

"Away! Away!"

Piper wasn't quite as successful hiding her laugh this time, and Dusi was already out the door. But I stood stubbornly in the threshold.

"You said you were here last night. Do you have anyone who can corroborate that?"

"Only the entire town! Has *anyone* ever seen me leave this place? No. Because I like it here. I don't like it," she gestured with the Pelican, "out there. Not anymore. I am selling this old rat trap and leaving. Now go away."

She slammed the door. Good thing I could move quickly, too.

We all stood on the leaky porch for a moment.

"That was amazing!" Piper said. "You were brilliant! Did you see how upset she got? Do you think she's the murderer? She sounds like the murderer. She hated him."

We headed back to the car. "Maybe," I said. "She said

she deserved to be the one to murder him. Is that a partial confession?”

“It could be,” Dusi said, ducking into the car. “Are you going to tell Delaney?”

Piper and I got in the car, too.

“I don’t have much to tell her yet. Marlene didn’t admit to killing him, just that she deserved to. She said winter killed him, and he stayed in the house in winter. Maybe she thinks the historical draft killed him.”

“Freezing to death?” Piper asked.

“Maybe? He said he was reading and someone came into the house. I’m not sure that her story and his line up.”

“And the noise upstairs?” Dusi asked.

“Yeah, I want to check into that,” I said.

“Do you think it’s Burgess?” Piper said. “Snuck up there and hiding out?”

“I don’t know. I think if he *were* there, he wouldn’t have let her smack talk him like that. He’d have to have his say.”

“Sounds like a no,” Dusi said.

“It’s a no with a side of I-want-to-check-it-out when she isn’t looking.”

Piper rubbed her hands together. “Okay, so who do we talk to next?”

“You both must have other things to do. Piper, you don’t get a lot of days off, and Dusi you’re in the middle of painting…”

“Are you kidding me?” Piper said. “This is the most fun I’ve had all month.” She glanced back at Dusi.

"West," Dusi said. "You should talk to West."

"Oh, I am so not doing that. Let's go talk to Clara. Find out if my old enemy has anything to do with his murder."

"I like the sound of that even better," Piper said.

So did I. Because, frankly, I wouldn't put it past that icy little witch to be the killer.

CHAPTER 8

"It's...nice," Piper said. "Sorry, Jules."

"Yeah," I sighed, "it is."

Dusi put her hand on my shoulder and squeezed in sympathy.

It wasn't that I wanted Clara's house, which she'd inherited from her grandmother, to be a dump but since I'd forgotten she owned a house in Ordinary, I was sort of hoping it would be a dump.

Instead, it was a cute cottage, with brown shingles and green trim. It had been kept up well, and used as a vacation rental for families.

A long straight walk led to the front door and enclosed porch, and a white picket fence ran from the curb to either side of the house. It was March, so not a lot of flowers had bloomed yet, but there was a pop of pink azaleas and the deep green of rhodies dotting the yard, along with a few brave daffodils.

A FOR SALE sign on a post in the middle of the well-maintained grass somehow made the place look chipper.

The rain had let up, heavy clouds conspiring eastward.

We walked down that long path and I knocked on the door.

The enclosed porch was almost all glass, and two large windows on the house bracketed the porch. It was no surprise she'd seen us coming.

Clara threw open the door. "Juley, it's horrible, just horrible!" She was red-eyed and blotchy-faced, her pale hair pulled back messily with a clip.

"Uh..." I said.

"Who would do such a thing?" She launched herself into my arms, and I *oof*ed from the impact.

From Piper's wide eyes, she was just as surprised as I was.

Dusi, however, slunk past us and headed into the house.

I gave her a thumbs up behind Clara's back. Maybe she could get in a little snooping.

"Someone must fix this," Clara sobbed. She straight-armed back, shifting her hold on my jacket. "You'll fix it. Juley you must. You are always so helpful. It's what you do. You help people."

The last thing I wanted to do was anything that helped or fixed Clara's...whatever this was.

"How about we go inside?" Piper asked.

"Yes," I grunted as I pried one of her hands off my arm. "You can tell us all about it inside."

Clara grabbed a fistful of my sleeve and held on like she was afraid a strong wind would blow me away.

"Fine," she sniffed, reaching out and gripping Piper just as tightly. "Let's go inside. I have…I think I have tea? I'm selling the place you know. It's why I'm back in town. I was going to let you make an offer on it…I told you I could make your life exciting…but you actually like living in that stupid, crowded little shop, don't you?"

"Oh for…yes," I said, annoyed. "I like my shop."

We made our way into the house—the doorway becoming a problem because Clara refused to let go of either of us. We got wedged in the doorway like a couple of pigeons trying to squeeze through a knothole.

"Stuck, stuck!" I said, leaning backward.

"Hang on." Piper shifted sideways. "I think I can—"

"Get in!" Clara gave us a huge tug.

We popped through the door faster than a pinched watermelon seed.

"There!" Clara (who was stronger than she looked) said breathing heavily. She still hadn't let go. When she got an idea in her head, she never gave up.

The first impression of the place I had was: white.

The ceiling came to a second-story peak with two huge skylights up there surrounded by white shiplap. The walls were painted white, the floor was white wood, and the furniture was white with white accents.

An open loft came out over half the living space, and beneath it was a kitchen (white) and a hallway down to the end of the house with doors on either side that would be bedrooms and a bathroom.

The whole place smelled of pine cleaning solution.

"Tea's in the kitchen."

"Are we all going together?" Piper asked.

Clara frowned at Piper, then at her hand on Piper's sleeve. She released her. "You. Go make it for us."

Piper shook her head and walked off to the kitchen. I hoped she was going to snoop, too.

Clara hauled me down onto the couch with her. "Jules, tell me you've heard."

I pulled my other arm free and when she made a go for it again, I tipped my head and gave her a look.

"My space," I said waving a finger around me. "Your space." I waved at her side of the couch.

She slumped her shoulders and turned the wad of tissue over and over in her hand. "Have you? Heard?"

"I have no idea what you're talking about. Why are you upset?"

"Do you remember our teacher? Mr. Carmichael? I mean you must because he *loved* you so much. Loved you more than any of us."

I laughed, nice and loud. "He hated me."

She frowned and searched my face. "No. He...*loved* you. You were his favorite. Not like me and West. Or his sister what's-her-name. He hated her, too. Always fighting over that house."

"He never liked anything I—" I stopped before I really got going on how wrong she was.

She was the student he chose over all of us because he said she was the strongest. *She* was the one he always asked to help with his "secret important work." *She* was the one he gave the most time to, the most attention to, and the most magical clout—crowning her the leader of our group who would carry out our mission if he were ever incapacitated.

Clara let that power over us, her peers, go to her head. She lured West away from me and shut Marlene out of our meetings until Marlene had had enough and never came back.

Clara was Burgess's choice for his successor. A bad one, but well, that was so many years ago, I'd had plenty of time to lie to myself that it had never bothered me.

"I came here to ask you what you know about Burgess' death," I said as evenly as I could.

"His death?" She wrung the tissue in her hands. "I wasn't...I don't know anything about his death. That was years ago. He just died."

"Do you know how? The cause? Were you in town when it happened?"

She took in a breath and let it out shakily. "Murder, I think." Her eyes went round and she pressed the tissue up to her mouth.

"Not that anyone proved it," she mumbled through her fingers. "But...it seemed suspicious that he fell out of his chair and hit his head." She pulled her hand away from her mouth.

"He'd lived in that house forever. How would he have suddenly forgotten how to get up out of his favorite chair?"

"Maybe someone pushed him," Piper said bringing in

the tea. She set the cups on the coffee table, but none of us reached for them.

"It would have had to be someone strong," Clara said. "Burgess wasn't a small man. It would take power to push him out of a chair hard enough to make him hit his head. And how would someone even know he was there? He was private and distrustful, don't you think, Juley?"

"Yes," Piper said. "What do you think, Jules?"

I thought that there was no way I was going to get chummy with Clara of all people by bonding over Burgess' death.

"Jules," Piper prompted, while looking sidelong at Clara. "Do you think Burgess could have been killed?"

Right. I was here to get info out of Clara.

"It's possible. If not someone pushing him, maybe... hitting him? You said it was a head injury?"

She drew in a breath then paused for a moment. I couldn't tell what she was looking for in my expression. If it was sympathy, she wasn't going to get it.

"I don't know. I just thought the whole thing sounded suspicious. Who falls over in their chair and dies?"

"How did you hear about his death? Where you in town then?"

She dabbed at her nose. "No. I wasn't living here, of course, but I'm sure someone mentioned it when I visited to check on the rental. Or...I don't know. It was such a shock to hear he had died, and now it's just...so much worse." Fresh tears trickled down her cheeks.

"Why is it worse?" I asked.

"Someone dug him up! His grave is..." she flapped her hand, "empty. And he's gone."

"Why do you think that?"

"There's a festival coming up, you know," she said, with enough bite to sound like her normal, horrible self. "Ladle-to-Grave? I wanted to see what was so special about the graveyard that people would want to tour it during a full moon. But it's blocked by police tape, and they're putting fences around half of it."

"But how'd you hear about an empty grave?" I pressed.

She did the hand-flapping again. "It's all over town."

"Do you have any idea why someone would dig up his grave?" Piper asked. "It's not like he had anything valuable buried with him, did he? Was he rich?"

Clara shrugged, and twisted her hair between her fingers. "No. I mean, maybe he'd been buried with something magical? Something with personal value?"

That was...an interesting leap.

"Like his token?" I asked.

"Yes!" She leaped forward to grab my sleeve again. I pushed her hand away. She didn't seem to notice.

"He loved the tokens, didn't he? Said they were the most powerful magic because they were so personal. I mean, I still have mine." She lifted her wrist.

Yep. The silver coin hanging from her bracelet had the world on one side and the star on the other.

"I know it's just a token," she went on, "but it

reminds me of such a good time in my life. In *our* lives. You were there, too, Juley. Do you still have yours?"

"Probably in a box somewhere." That was a lie. I'd buried it under the front threshold to my shop. The magic in it helped keep my shop safe, cozy, and mine.

"Well, you should look for it," she insisted. "To keep you safe. Because there's something I haven't told you."

She pressed her lips together and looked around like she expected someone to jump out of a closet with a knife.

The sound of a door closing with a quiet snick made Piper and I exchange a look. It was probably Dusi, letting herself out through the back.

Clara started to turn her head that way, but I grabbed her sleeve.

"What is it?" I asked a little too loudly. "What were you going to tell me? I am so very interested in everything you have to say."

Her eyes went wide and I thought she was trying to whisper, but it sounded like a balloon releasing a thin stream of air. "He might not be dead!"

She was watching for my reaction, so I did my best to look shocked, then skeptical. "Why wouldn't he be dead?"

"You know how he used to give me private lessons because I am better than the rest of you?"

"Yes," I said through gritted teeth.

"He told me he was never going to die. And if someone killed him, he would rise from the dead to get his revenge—during a full moon—the Worm Moon! His grave is dug up and it's March, which means the Worm Moon is Saturday. Do you think he did it? Do you think he rose from the dead?"

She was saying all the right things, well, things that made sense, I supposed, considering magic and Burgess were involved.

But I was getting weird vibes off her. Her mix of fear and fascination made it seem like she was giddy about the situation. As if she wanted him to be on the loose, undead, and hungry for revenge.

"I don't know if he could raise himself from the dead."

"Maybe someone helped him."

"I suppose that's possible. But who? Who can cast that kind of dark magic? A necromancer?"

"West did it!" she blurted. She scrambled off the couch, wringing her hands. "I know he did. He hated Burgess. He murdered him and now he's stolen Burgess's token and wants to use it to become immortal!"

"Wow," Piper whispered. "Didn't see that coming."

"Clara, calm down, take a breath," I said. "Let's start at the beginning. Where were you last night?"

"What?"

"Late. After midnight. Where were you?"

"I was here. I mean, I took a walk because I always take a walk when I can't sleep, but I was here."

"Is there anyone who could verify that? Anyone who saw you on your walk?"

"In Ordinary? This boring little town?"

"Where did you go?" Piper asked. "On your walk."

She drew her chin up and glared at Piper, then me. "I knew I couldn't trust you to believe me. You think because we weren't friendly when we were young, that I'm a terrible person. I shouldn't have said any of this. You need to go. You both need to go right now."

She wiggled her fingers and magic pushed me. It felt like really pokey fingers stabbing into my back. She wanted us to leave, her magic wanted us to leave, and it would have taken more effort (and bigger magic than I'm allowed to use in Ordinary) to shut her down and push back.

She stomped over to the door and held it open. "Good-bye. Go away. Don't tell West I said anything, or else."

"Or else?" I asked.

"You heard me. Or else."

"Thanks for your time." Piper stood. "Good luck selling the house."

We were magic perp-walked to the door. Piper left first, marching toward the car.

I lingered on the porch. Maybe it was because I hadn't gotten much sleep. Or maybe all those lies I'd told myself that her ruining my life years ago didn't matter had finally caught up to me. But right now, I wanted to upset her life a little, too.

"There's something I haven't told you," I said. "I think you're right. Burgess is out there," I pointed behind me, "looking for who killed him. Looking for someone to punish unless they admit what they did to him. So, if you remember anything, if you know anything about how he was revived, you need to come clean."

Her face rolled through quick emotions: fear, surprise, then raw hatred that took me back.

She laughed.

"Are you accusing me of raising him from the dead? How childish. Get over yourself, Juley. You've never understood how real magic works." Her magic gave one last shove and she slammed the door.

"And you've always underestimated me," I muttered, heading toward the car.

"She's quite an experience," Piper noted.

"So is rabies."

She laughed and gave me a quick one-arm hug. "I don't think we got very much out of her. Sorry I messed it up asking her where she went walking."

"You did not mess it up. You forced her to not answer, and that can mean something, too."

"True," Piper said as we got in the car where Dusi was waiting. "She admitted she knew he was undead and accused West of knocking him out of his chair. That's something."

"That is something," Dusi agreed.

I pulled my seatbelt and clicked it into place. "I don't think it's the truth, though. She's a liar. Always has been. She's lying about some of what she told us. Or all of it."

"Did you find anything?" Piper asked Dusi.

"Only that her taste in decorating means using every shade of white on the planet. Bedrooms and bathrooms were cleaned by a maid service. You can tell the house has been used as a vacation rental. It doesn't feel lived in at all."

"There was nothing strange in the house?" I asked, a lot less excited about this whole solving-the-mystery thing.

"Nothing in the rooms I could access. The door to the basement was locked. I didn't have a chance to try to force it open before you all came in."

"Locked basements are pretty common in a rental," Piper said.

"True," Dusi agreed. "What's our next move?"

They were waiting for me to answer, even though they must have already figured out the next logical step. We had to talk to the other witch in town who knew Burgess. We had to talk to West.

"West," I said.

"Yep," Piper said.

"Agreed," Dusi said.

"And I think we can do that later," I said.

"Jules," they said at the same time.

"I will. *We* will. But I need to get back to the shop. Marty's shift is almost over. And I haven't had lunch, and I still need to set up for the festival. We all have to hang silver moons and stars and lights. So, I know I—*we*—need to talk to him. But not yet."

They were quiet. "When?" Dusi finally asked.

"Tonight?"

"Tonight works," Piper said. "Or you know, maybe earlier, but you just let us know how that goes, okay?"

"How what goes? Lunch?" I asked, starting the car.

Piper just laughed.

CHAPTER 9

Marty was still at the shop, but I knew he had to leave soon for his shift at the hardware store.

"You can head on out," I said, bustling into the main room. "Sorry it took me so long."

"Not a problem. I've got the rest of the day off. I can stay for a while. I mean someone has to handle this huge rush of customers."

There were no customers in the shop.

"How thoughtful of you," I said, tidying a small display of books by the window.

"I live to serve. How's your day been?"

"I just saw Dusi," I said.

"Uh-huh," he said like everything in him wasn't interested in what I was about to say.

"She's almost done painting her house."

"Good?"

"It is good. As soon as it's done, she'll be settled in. Have a place of her own. Maybe be looking for something to do. Like go out to coffee with a certain nephew of mine.”

“Ah. And now we change the subject. What were you and Dusi doing today? Stirring up trouble?”

“No. Of course not. What are you working on?” I nodded at the computer screen and the free realtor brochure next to him.

He grinned, having caught me in a subject change of my own. “I’m just looking into what kind of spaces are available in town.”

“For your gaming group?”

“That, yes. Ever since I talked to you about it, I can’t get the idea of a board game café out of my head. Not that I’m going to do anything immediately. It’s just…I like the idea of creating a community space.”

“I wish I could give you more space here. You know I would if I could.”

“No, that’s not what I want. I love the shop. I can’t imagine Ordinary without it. I’m just thinking about a someday, not about today.”

“Well, let me know if I can help. I’d be happy to ask around.”

“Still in the planning stages.” He clicked to another screen. “But I’ll keep you in the know.”

I rearranged the witchy coffee mugs and bells near the window. Something outside caught my eye. There, on the other side of the street, in the late afternoon light stood West Heath. He had one hand in his pocket and was looking at my shop like it was a crossword he was only one clue away from solving.

"Is that—" Marty started.

"I totally forgot something. Upstairs. The stove. It's on. Thank you for covering the shop." I rushed toward the back.

"Auntie," Marty's voice was caught somewhere between laughter and wonder. "I've never seen you run from anyone before."

I spun, and couldn't help myself—I laughed. "Take that back. I am not running. I am walking quickly."

His eyebrows shot up. "I've never seen you walk quickly to hide from anyone, either."

"I'm not hiding, I'm just going to be busy somewhere else. Out of sight where no one can find me."

Marty craned his neck to look out the window. "Who is that good-looking fellow out there? Is he new in town?"

"He's nobody. Just...nobody."

"All right. Nobody's crossing the street—long stride he's got. Uh-oh, he's at the door. Whatever will we do..."

West opened the door, setting off the little chime above it.

He scanned the space looking for something, his shoulders tight, his mouth turned down. When he saw me, everything in him relaxed.

What? I thought. *He thought I wouldn't be at my own shop?*

"Hello, Jules." His voice was warm and welcoming as a hearth fire in a storm. He wiped boots on the mat then stepped into the shop, closing the door behind him. "I hoped I'd see you here."

"West," I breathed.

"Afternoon," Marty said.

West seemed surprised there was another person in the store but nodded toward Marty. "Afternoon. This is nice." He moved slowly between the shelves, lingering at displays of crystals and cauldrons, spell pots, herbs, intention bottles and other magical items .

He picked up a very nice amethyst and turned it in his hand. He could sense the magic within it, I was sure. He acknowledged it and left it unbothered for the next person to find.

He moved toward the candles I loved because a local druid had made them from the wax from her bee hives. His eyebrows rose at the care and connection to nature woven through them.

Then he came my way.

"I like it," he said. "It feels like you."

And oh, there was the smile I'd tried to tell myself I'd forgotten.

It made me want to smile back at him, made me want to ask him where he had been all these years. Ask him why he'd disappeared.

But he'd come back to town on the same day our old teacher had been dug up. He wasn't just a blast from my past, he was a suspect. Grave robber. Maybe even a murderer if Clara was to be believed.

"Thank you," I managed.

"Is this a reading room?" He strolled to the space in the corner with beaded curtains closing it off from the rest of the shop. "Tarot?"

"Yes, I do Tarot readings." I lifted my chin. "It isn't a joke."

"I didn't think it was." He reached for his wallet. "You've always had amazing intuition. How much?"

"What?"

He waved at the beaded curtains. "For a reading?"

"I...um..."

Marty chimed in with our rates, then told West he could ring him up for it.

I threw a dirty look at my meddling nephew, but it slid right off him because he liked sticking his nose into other people's business, and no, I had no idea where he might have gotten that from.

"She's free now," Marty said. "I mean, unless you have that urgent thing you needed to take care of?"

Why was I still standing here? Why hadn't I moved, run—I mean, walked quickly—out of here, up the stairs where I didn't have to deal with this? Didn't have to deal with him?

"If you have time," West said, "I would love a reading."

There were no other customers in the shop, no ringing phone, no deliveries waiting to be unpacked.

Marty was pretending he was busy at the computer, mostly so he could eavesdrop.

I knew I could say no. I didn't need an excuse to say no.

I could refund him his money.

But there was a part of me that desperately wanted

to know more about where he had been, why he was here, and what was coming in his future.

A Tarot reading would give me some of that information.

It didn't have to be personal. He wasn't asking me out on a date. He just wanted to use my scrying abilities and my intuition.

"Shall we?" he asked, one step closer to the reading room. "Or should I come back at a better time?"

The idea of having to go through this indecision all over again, made up my mind. I wasn't a person who hesitated. I just dug right in and got things done.

I chuckled. "No. Now is good. Let's do this. Right this way, Mr. Heath."

I pushed the beads out of the way and stepped into the area, taking my place on one side of the small round table.

"Just West," he said following me through.

I loved this space, with its draped scarves across the ceiling and tiny soft yellow lights twinkling through them. The table was rich cherry wood, polished to a shine, with the zodiac inlaid in gold, and the planets, represented by stones and crystals, scattered across it.

The chairs were comfortable, and crystals, plants, and little magical items were cozied into the corners.

"All right, West." I said. "Get comfortable."

He made a sound that could have meant anything and stopped with his hand on the back of the other chair. "Here?"

I nodded.

He sat, and it was just the two of us in this intimate space.

"You look good, Jules. I meant to say that before."

"You look like you paid for a Tarot reading," I said. "So, let's just do that, shall we?"

He sat back and spread his hands. "Absolutely."

He had good hands. They were big, and the backs of them carried a couple scars that he never would say how he'd gotten. But for hands that big, that powerful, he was careful with how he touched the things around him, and was, in every way, surprisingly gentle.

For a possible grave robber and murderer, my brain reminded me.

Right. Time to get to work.

"Clear your mind," I said, easing into the familiarity of beginning a session. "Breathe deeply and center yourself in this moment. We are welcoming spirit to join us, and to help show us the truths we most need to hear."

West shifted in the chair a bit, and his shoe touched mine. I locked gazes with him and his slow grin spread wider. I drew my foot away.

"I welcome spirit," West said quietly, holding eye contact, "to join us and show us our best and most needed messages, information, and wisdom in light and love and truth. I welcome spirit to enlighten us and guide us toward our best lives, our best selves, our best choices."

It was suddenly hot in the little room. I really should install a fan in here one of these days. I lifted my eyebrows, letting him know it was going to take more than a few pretty words and that smolder to fluster me.

He made a little moue with his lips, then tucked a smile into the corner of his mouth.

I chose a deck of cards from the shelf next to me, trusting magic to lead me to the deck that would be the most appropriate.

It was a small deck with bright yellow card backs tiled with colorful little bear-shaped creatures.

I shuffled, cut, then placed three cards face down on the table.

"Gummy Bear Tarot," West said trying to sound serious and losing the battle. "Going for the big guns, aren't you, Jules?"

I laughed. "Do you have something against the oracle powers of Gummy Bears?"

"No, not at all. Mad respect. Not everyone can handle a deck with that kind of power."

"They give very good readings," I insisted.

"I believe you."

"Brutally honest readings."

"Candy tells no lies."

"West, I'm not joking. These Gummy Bears deliver a wallop."

"I like that."

"Wallops?"

"You saying my name."

"Let's just see what the cards have to say." I flipped the first card over. "Your recent past. Death. How do you like that wallop?"

"Bracing," he said.

"That's your past. Death. You've seen an ending, something that maybe you wanted very much has not come to pass or was taken from you."

"Or someone died," he said.

The tarot wasn't always literal. After so many years of readings, I knew the death card could mean rebirth. I mean, yes, the Death card could indicate an ending of life, but actually it told of transformation. Of letting go of one thing or letting something end so you could move on to something more, something better.

But since I needed to find out if he knew anything about the grave robbing and undead guy, I was happy to go along with his interpretation.

"Yes," I said. "It can mean someone died in your past. Maybe a mentor. Someone you respected and looked up to. Like Burgess Carmichael."

All the teasing, the flirting, the smolder, and easy-going vibe disappeared.

"That old conman? He wasn't a mentor. He was a user. His class with the whole we're-so-much-better-than-other-witches he was teaching? It was all lies."

"All of it?"

"Enough of it. He preyed on our hopes and insecurities. He liked seeing us struggle, found every way he could to make us turn on each other. Kept secrets. Nothing we did was ever good enough for him and his quest to take over the world."

"He didn't really want to take over the world."

"Oh, yes, he did. I hated how he took something good

—magic, friendship—and turned it into something so vile."

"I knew you were frustrated with him back then, but are you telling me you hated him, West?"

"Let's just say I didn't shed any tears when he died."

"You mean when someone broke into his house and pushed him off his chair?"

"He deserved to be pushed off a chair. He deserved to be pushed off a cliff." His eyes went wide and he leaned farther away, rubbing at his jaw. "That was harsh of me. I have some…unprocessed issues with him. With what he wanted to do with magic."

"What did he want to do? And don't say take over the world. How was he going to do that? The world's a pretty big place."

He blinked. "You really don't know?"

"I was not one of the popular kids. Obviously."

"You were the best of us."

"Could have fooled me. Before you argue—this isn't about me. This is about Burgess. How was he trying to take over the world?"

He shifted in the chair, and his gaze dropped to the Death card. "Death was a part of it. His, if you can believe it. All of ours. The spell he was trying to create would have been fueled by all of our magic cast together.

"The full moon, the Worm Moon, had something to do with it. Someone had to be raised from the grave. Maybe more than one person? I don't remember." He shook his head. "It was dark magic. He never told me the details of what the spell would do, how it would allow him to take over the world. Frankly, I didn't stay around long enough to find out."

"No," I said, "you didn't stay around at all."

His gaze flicked up at the annoyance in my tone. He nodded.

I took a breath to clear old emotions. I didn't have time for them. There was a murder to solve.

"Where were you when he died?"

"Here. In Ordinary. With Clara."

"You were both here? Together?" I wish I didn't sound so surprised.

"You remember," he said. "Burgess called us all to get back together. Said he'd figured out how to cast the final spell that would 'change the world'." He bent his fingers once to put those words in quotes. "Without using dark magic, which he had sworn off of."

"That's when I found he wanted to raise the dead and become immortal, if I'm remembering this correctly. Instead of dark magic, he needed all of our tokens for it. I told him he could kick rocks. He was furious when you didn't show up. Without you, without us all together, his spell would not work."

"How did—I didn't even know there was a meeting —no one told me."

"Probably better that way," he said. "That was the last time I saw Clara, by the way. In case you wanted to know. I hadn't seen her for years before then, and until yesterday, I still hadn't. She's selling her house. She said she'd cut me a good deal if I wanted to buy it. I've been thinking about moving to somewhere with a slower pace. Somewhere by water. Like Ordinary."

"That's—it's none of my business where you move. And I don't care why you're with Clara." Okay, that last part was a lie.

He pointed at the cards. "What's next?"

I turned over the remaining two cards. "In your present, Judgement. In your near future, the Seven of Swords."

He stared at the cards. I stared at the cards.

"Death, Judgement, Seven of swords." His blue eyes rose to mine and there was genuine curiosity there. "What do you make of that?"

"There are many ways to read these," I stalled.

I could tell him someone in his life was judging him, or I could tell him Judgement was also a card asking him to transform, to rise above the life he was living and to reach for something more spiritual. Judgement was a calling. Judgement wanted him to become more of who he wanted to be. More than he had ever dreamed he could be.

I could tell him the seven of swords meant he needed to do something—maybe everything—differently. In ways other people wouldn't have thought of doing it. To march to the beat of his own magical drum while keeping his actions and decisions hidden for now.

I could tell him that card could mean he was sneaking around and trying to not get caught doing something he shouldn't be doing, or that someone else was sneaking around behind his back, trying to steal something from him.

Lots of choices. So I read the cards as clearly as I could.

I pointed at Judgement. "You need to decide who you want to be. Something is calling you to your best good, and you need to answer that call. Stop messing around and make your life what you want it to be. Life is finite, West. None of us are immortal, no matter how young we pretend to be. Listen to your heart and do what you know is right."

Like maybe confess to killing Burgess, I thought.

"Seven of Swords in your future. Welp. Someone is going behind your back. They want to steal something very important from you. You have an enemy you might not think is your enemy. They want what you have. So while you're trying to reach your goals, you need to guard your back."

Yes, it was blunt, but that's what the cards said. I'd given it to him as straight as I could.

He'd gone awfully quiet.

I looked away from the cards and studied his reaction. All the color had drained from his face.

"That's...that's a lot, Jules. It could mean...it could mean a lot of things. I need to go." He stood a little too quickly, a little gracelessly.

The reading had more than spooked him. It had shaken him to his core.

"West," I said, "wait."

"I need to go." He hurried out, the beads clattering and swinging behind him.

CHAPTER 10

"It's Marlene." I wiggled my fingers to cool the tea and took a sip.

The Puffin Muffin was busy today. We'd grabbed the last spot even though that meant the three of us were crowded around a table made for two.

Dusi's snakes were covered by a lovely blue and green scarf. She wore octagonal mirrored sunglasses and looked so much more relaxed than when she'd returned to town a month or so ago. She was nibbling on one of the best almond and cardamom biscotti ever baked.

Tufa was curled up in the kangaroo purse on her lap. She'd somehow gotten him to leave his paper towel treasure behind today.

Piper stared out the window, like she was watching something on the far horizon coming our way.

Her hair was braided back, and she wore another one of her hand-knits—a white cabled cardigan—over a lime-colored top and jeans. Her latte steamed next to a hefty slice of chocolate chip pie which she'd eaten from the crust toward the point.

"Why Marlene?" Dusi asked. "I thought Clara was the worst person in your old coven."

"Not a coven, just a class. Believe me, I *want* it to be Clara. She's never been a friend—and that is the nicest thing I can say about her."

"You can say something that isn't nice." Piper looked away from the window. "It's just us."

"All right. She's a manipulative, petty, mean-spirited old crone. And I'm an old crone, too, so I can call it as I see it."

Dusi grinned—something I always loved seeing— and Piper laughed loudly enough she had to slap her hand over her mouth because the people crammed around the table next to us stared.

"That's the spirit," Piper said. "Feel better?"

"Actually, I do. But I still think Marlene killed him."

"I can see how she'd have the opportunity," Dusi said. "She would have known when he was at the house. What was her motivation?"

"Well, she said he was a bully. She didn't like him. She probably wanted the house full time. Do I need a third? She buried him with a bird on his head."

"Petty revenge to the end," Piper agreed.

"Sibling hatred can be the worst," Dusi said.

"But let's turn that question on Clara," Piper said. "Didn't she hate Burgess?"

"No. Not at all. He gave her all his attention. Thought she was the best witch of the group. And, while I hate to admit it, she did seem upset that he was dead and that his grave had been robbed."

"Which could be an act," Dusi said.

"It could be," I agreed. "But if Clara was the killer, she would had to have known when he was home and then sneak in and knock him out of his chair and leave him and…I don't know. She doesn't live here, Marlene does. Clara hasn't been back in what, thirty years?"

"She has the rental house," Piper said. "She could have stayed here a lot over the years."

"A rental company takes care of the house, so she never has to check in on it. I don't think she's the kind of person who would want to stay in Ordinary. Too many rules she wouldn't want to follow."

"But we agree it's strange she came back now," Dusi said. "When the grave was robbed and your dead teacher was raised."

I nodded. "It's strange both Clara and West were in town when that happened."

"Let's stick to Clara," Piper said. "She came to town, dug up the grave, raised Burgess from the dead then… just left him there? Why? What did she do all that work for?"

"His token?" Dusi asked. "Isn't that what she thought someone might be looking for?"

"I wish I'd asked him if he'd had it on him when I had the chance," I muttered.

Dusi dusted biscotti crumbs off her fingers. "Any luck with the invisibility spell?"

"No. As far as I can tell, it hasn't wavered. I told you I made it strong."

"What if there was another reason to dig him up?" Piper asked. "Something that doesn't involve witchery?"

"You mean a regular grave robbing?" I asked. "How deliciously mundane."

"It isn't only supernaturals who live in town," Dusi said. "Mortals can murder, too."

"Huh." I thought about it. Lots of people committed crimes for reasons that had nothing to do with magic.

Ordinary wasn't a hotbed of serious crime, but we'd had our share of non-law-abiding citizens. People who kidnapped and hid Mrs. Yates' penguin might be the kind who would let Mr. Bandy's pigs out in the middle of the night.

But would they get it in their head to dig up a grave? Was it just a coincidence they'd chosen Burgess's grave?

"But the idea that it's a non-magical crime falls apart when we add in raising someone from the dead," Dusi said. "I don't think any non-magical person could raise a person from the dead, and if they did, I don't think they'd just leave them behind, would they?"

"How about we look at things this way," I suggested. "Who benefits from Burgess being alive?"

We were quiet. Piper finished off her cookie pie, while I drank my tea.

"Yeah," I said, "I got nothing."

"Okay, what do we think about West as a suspect?" Piper asked. "I like him by the way, but there are plenty of charming killers out there."

I laughed. "Charming killers?"

"Hey, I watch the true crime shows. I see how far charisma can get a person. West, he has charisma."

"And a good smile," Dusi added.

"Did you see those arms?" Piper put in gleefully. "And his voice? We should go talk to him now."

"I did a Tarot reading for him." At their stunned expressions, I said, "He paid for it. And Marty was there watching the shop, and well, I did a Tarot reading. And asked him some questions."

"What did the cards say?" Dusi asked. "For that matter, what did *he* say?"

The Puffin Muffin suddenly seemed even more crowded. A kid ran into the place, tugging his adult, who was arguing on their phone about types of electric lawn mowers.

The folks at the table next to us were ranking which comedy show was the best, and in the coveted window seats, the local crochet group, the C.O.C.K.S. were cackling away, elbows out, yarn spooling from bags and laps and bowls.

The door opened again and the place went quiet for a moment before returning to normal volume. The person responsible for that pause in conversation had spotted us and was walking our way.

"Uh-oh," Piper said. "Here we go."

Bertie, who was a Valkyrie and also the powerhouse community organizer who put on every dang festival in the town, was a vision. She appeared to be in her eighties, had short white hair with razor straight bangs, pale skin, and piercing green eyes. Her business suit was a lovely shade of plum, which she'd highlighted with gold jewelry studded with amethyst and garnet.

Next to her was the gilman, Chris Lagon, who was the owner of Jump Off Jack brewery and restaurant. He had long dark hair, dark skin, and tattoos that covered the subtle scales on the back of his hands, arms, and across his neck. He smiled and lifted two fingers in a wave.

"Jules," Bertie said, stopping at our table. "Marty said you might be here. I need you to take on a larger part of the Ladle-to-Grave event."

"I...uh, yes. Of course. What do you need me to do?"

"There has been a change to the graveyard tour. One area of the grounds with the best ghost stories is now a part of a crime scene, as you well know."

"I didn't dig him up," I said with a laugh.

"He's invisible, yes?" Chris asked quietly, just a smidge of his Louisianan accent flavoring his words.

"Yes. That's my fault. I don't have a spell that can find him, either. But it will wear off. Eventually."

He chuckled. "I love this town. Carry on," he said to Bertie.

"I am not interested in the missing person," she said. "I am diverting the flow of traffic for the event. It will now start at Jump Off Jack's or alternatively at Fool Moon. The map will outline the routes through partici-pating businesses. I want both of you to strongly suggest the graveyard tour be taken with a guide, for the ease of parking, and also because the guide is trained in all the legends and lore."

"People were going to walk the graveyard alone?" Piper asked.

"People enjoy breaking rules," Bertie said. "So of course they were going to walk it alone. Instructing them not to won't solve the matter, but I will have guides stationed at the graveyard gates and outside each of your businesses to take groups through the graveyard every half hour."

"Okay," I said, "I can make sure there's hot beverages available, and I'll put a few chairs out front. Do you have the maps?"

"I've left a box of them at your shop."

Bertie was nothing if not efficient.

"Chris, do you have a festival menu I should hand out?"

"I'm printing them now. I'll drop them off before Friday."

"Good. I'll have Marty swing by with some of my sales flyers. And...how'd we do?" I asked Bertie.

She had her phone in her hand and was tapping the screen. "Excellently. Thank you for your cooperation."

"Happy to do my part to make your sister eat crow," Chris said.

Bertie's sharp gold nails paused over her phone. She looked up at him. "What have you heard about Robyn?"

"Only that she's running a Midnight Snack and Moonwalk this weekend and told her local paper she was going to pull in twice the traffic as 'shabby old Ordinary's rinky-dink festival'."

Bertie's expression didn't change, but an intensity rolled off of her. I blinked and swore I saw the afterglow of huge gold wings behind her.

"Did she?" The way she said it made me thankful I wasn't her sister.

Chris just nodded. "She did, but I have no doubt the best warrior will win."

"Yes," Bertie said, redoubling her screen tapping. "I will." She tapped one last time and tucked her phone into her pocket.

Then she speared me with a look. "Thank you for doing your part. If you have concerns, tell me."

With that she turned and strode out into the weather, the phone already at her ear.

Chris exhaled. "Well, that was fun, wasn't it?" He rubbed his hands together, gaze lifted to the menu over the counter. "I think I need a stiff coffee. See you all around."

"Bye," Piper said.

"Thanks, Chris," I added.

Dusi, as was her way, didn't say anything until he was out of earshot. "The cards? The tarot reading?"

I regrouped and told them about West's reading.

"Uh…" Piper said, "that's not great? Walking out in a rush. Did he look guilty?"

"Maybe. Shocked for sure," I said.

"Do you think he murdered Burgess and brought him back to life?" Dusi asked.

"If he were in Ordinary and had the opportunity? I suppose he could have had the motivation to kill him."

"What does your intuition say?" Piper asked. "What does your heart say?"

"They say too much, which is why I can't trust them. Not when it comes to him. I don't want to believe West would kill someone. But I don't know him anymore. Not who he is now."

"We are always…" Piper shook her head. "I like to think that we remain who we always have been. Some people lean into their worst tendencies, or make mistakes, even terrible mistakes. But if we are kind-hearted to begin with, I think we carry that through our lives."

"And if we're angry, or carry enough hatred," Dusi said, "that remains a part of us, too."

"I don't know why he's in town," I admitted. "He said Clara was trying to sell him her house, but should I believe that? He's strong enough to dig up a grave. I don't know that Clara or Marlene could do that on their own. He would be strong enough to knock Burgess off his chair, too."

"Could magic instead of brute force have done those things?" Piper asked.

"Possibly, but the grave looked like it was shovel work."

"Does West hate Burgess enough to go to that extreme?" Dusi asked.

"West was Burgess's second favorite. Before yesterday, I would have told you West looked up to him. But he was bitter yesterday, disillusioned by what Burgess had done, what he'd tried to teach us. He's still mad about what Burgess did to our class all those years ago."

"What was that?" Piper asked. "I mean, if it's not a secret?"

I waved my hand like it was nothing. "Burgess had a theory that if the five of us chose two arcana icons and poured our magic into them—via our tokens—then joined them together under a full moon—I think the Worm Moon—we would be able to generate a power that would make us immortal. I guess he thought he could then take over the world, though I don't know how."

They were silent.

"Did you want to be immortal?" Dusi asked.

"I was so young. Back then, it seemed like it would be fun, living forever. But now, well, I can't complain that my life has been enhanced and extended by magic, but every season has an end, doesn't it?"

They nodded.

"Not that it matters. Burgess never cast the immortality spell. He realized the magic skewed too dark—someone had to die for it, or maybe everyone had to die for it to work—and as far as I know, he dropped it flat."

"How does killing people make someone immortal?" Piper asked.

"He never went into the details of the spell—well, not with me. But the cost of that magic was high enough he abandoned it completely. He shifted our studies to brewing potions. I actually liked that better." I lifted my tea. "I got pretty good at it."

"So, what's our next step?" Piper asked. "Talk to Marlene again and see if she'll confess to murdering her brother?"

"It wouldn't hurt trying one more time," I said. "Even if she doesn't confess, maybe she'll give us an idea of where Burgess might be. She might know his old hideouts."

"Oh, shoot," Piper said, like she'd forgotten something. "I don't think I can go."

Her phone rang and she swiped the screen to read a message.

"Yeah, they need me to cover a shift. I'll work until after the dinner rush. Can you wait until I'm done?"

I opened my mouth, but she cut me off. "You're not going to, are you?"

"Ooooo, look at you using that seer ability to predict the future."

"My seer ability and that absolutely guilty look on your face."

I laughed. "I'll just go knock on her door. It'll be fine."

"Besides," Dusi said, "I'm coming with you."

"Didn't you tell me you wanted to get some of your art framed so you could hang in it the community center and in my shop for the festival?"

"I'd be happy to hang it in your shop. But my art can wait." She shrugged. "We're friends. And friends don't let friends question cranky old witches in drafty old mansions alone."

Q

THE ROOKERY DIDN'T LOOK NEARLY AS HAUNTED IN THE BRIGHT sunshine as it had when we'd first stopped in, but it did look a lot more run down.

Tufa was sniffing around the edges of the porch, and making little sneeze noises. I rang the bell and waited.

And waited.

"Do you think she has a camera out here and just doesn't want to let us in?" I asked.

Dusi shook her head. "I don't see any electronics. Maybe she's too deep into the house to hear the bell. Or she's sleeping."

It was after noon, but a nap could be a possibility.

"Do you want me to pick the lock?" Dusi offered.

Tufa squeaked and came running, always ready for mischief.

"I love you for that," I said, "but let's try it first." I jiggled the handle (threw a little magic at it, too) and voila! The door swung open.

"Magic?" Dusi asked.

"Just to oil the hinges."

"She's going to call Delaney to report a breaking and entering."

"Well, then she should have answered the door. We're just two concerned citizens, concerned about her health."

Dusi huffed a little laugh and waved me forward. "Delaney will never buy that. Come on. Let's be concerned."

I pushed the door and Tufa bolted into the place.

The inside of the house looked...better. Slices of sunlight cut through the shades, casting warm, golden light. In the sitting area, several windows lit up the birds in the entryway, on the walls, and on the ceiling.

Well, they lit up what was left of the birds.

The birds had been torn apart, feathers and beaks and feet everywhere, as if someone had chopped them to bits and tossed them like a salad.

This wasn't good, I thought. *Oh, this wasn't good at all.*

"Marlene?" I called out, stepping over a flock of headless ducks to enter the sitting room.

Dusi sucked in a breath, and I stopped in my tracks.

Because right there, in the middle of the bird-littered rug, was Marlene.

She was lying on the floor, absolutely buried in bird bits.

She wasn't moving. Because she was dead.

CHAPTER 11

"How are you holding up?" Sage asked.

I was sitting outside the Rookery, Tufa, curled in my lap, an extra coat over my shoulders keeping me warm.

Dusi sat next to me, her fingers steady and reassuring on my arm. Her hand was warm and strong—she was a sculptor, after all. I forgot that sometimes.

"I'm okay. I think I'm okay." My voice came out soft and quiet, like it wasn't even mine.

Was I in shock?

Marlene hadn't been in my life for so many years. I'd spent decades not even thinking of her.

But seeing her dead, covered in all those feathers, had shaken me.

She had been a part of my past. Her sudden end made me wish I'd done something to help her. Made me wish I'd come here earlier and had stopped whoever had done this to her and her birds.

"We don't have a lot of these kinds of deaths in Ordinary." Sage was crouched on her heels in front of me, wearing her EMT uniform. "It's normal to be upset. Do you want me to call Marty to stay with you tonight?"

"I'll stay with her," Dusi said.

I blinked and found myself already shaking my head. "No, I'll be fine. I *am* fine. I just feel like if I'd come over here earlier, maybe..."

Tufa peeped and patted my arm, burrowing his little round head between my arm and side.

"No maybe about it," Sage said kindly. "She's been gone since last night. Trust me, I have a good sense for when a person's heart stops beating. Even if you'd shown up a little bit earlier, it wouldn't have made a difference."

"Can you tell how?" I asked. "I mean, was it violent? It looks violent. No one deserves that."

Sage's eyes sharpened with vampiric focus, and she lowered her voice. "I shouldn't share this before the coroner does her report, but yes. It's a blow to the back of her head. Either she fell, or someone snuck up and clobbered her."

Somehow, I'd known that. Known she hadn't died of a heart attack or in some other less murdery way. The back of my brain, the part that still had wheels that could turn beneath the weight of the shock, wondered who would do that to her, and why they had damaged her birds?

Could Marlene herself have torn them all apart? Or had someone else done it after finding her dead?

Why would someone tear up her birds?

Who would be so angry with her they wanted to destroy everything?

Well, not everything. The rest of the house seemed untouched. It was just the birds that had been ravaged.

Tufa made a funny half-growl, half-purr sound. He popped his head back out of where he'd wedged it under my arm, turned a circle in my lap, and yawned.

I petted his soft fur, and he peeped in approval.

Delaney strode over to us and stood there, looking down at me. I had a strange moment feeling like our roles in the world had been swapped, of being small in front of her, like she was the grown up, the authority figure who would help me navigate this uncertain situation, instead of me being her senior and guide.

"Auntie." She glanced at Sage and Dusi, her clear blue eyes missing nothing. "How are you doing?"

"I'm okay. I'm fine. It's just...I wish...It's pretty awful."

"I know." She looked at the house.

The wind picked up, stirring tendrils of hair that had gotten loose from her braid. Then she looked at the clouds.

It was going to rain soon. Live in Oregon long enough and you get pretty good at predicting it.

"I need you to go over everything with me again," she said. "Do you want to come down to the station to do that, or I'd be happy to take you home and we could do it there."

"I'd rather go home."

Tufa lifted his nose and peeped again.

"I'll take her." Dusi rose and helped me to my feet. I dug in my purse for my keys and handed them to her.

"I shouldn't let you two off alone," Delaney said.

"You've questioned both of us separately already," Dusi said. "We aren't going to change our answers just because we are in a car together."

"Jules?" Delaney asked.

"There is no reason for me to lie to you, honey. And if you think I have, I give you permission to have someone cast a truth spell on me."

Her eyes narrowed, but she nodded. Agreeing to a truth spell was no small thing. "All right. Go straight home. I'll be there in a few minutes."

Dusi picked up Tufa and guided me to the car. I got in the passenger seat while Tufa made himself at home on my lap again and Dusi settled into the driver's seat.

"How are you really doing?" She asked once she had navigated between emergency vehicles down the steep, narrow road.

"I'm in shock a little," I said honestly. "I know people die. I've seen death. But even though Sage said Marlene was hit on the head, there was just so much more violence in that room. Hatred."

"All those stuffed birds."

"Destroyed. Someone took the time to rip their insides out. Who does that?"

"Someone who hates taxidermy?"

"Maybe," I said, even though that didn't feel quite right. "Something...I don't know." I pressed my fingers to my eyes and was surprised at how cold they were.

"I thought she had done it," I said. "I really thought she had raised Burgess from the grave to get her revenge. To steal from him something he'd taken from her."

"Her chinchilla dust?" Dusi suggested.

That made me chuckle. "Something like that. But if she was the killer, then why is she dead? And if she's the one who brought Burgess back to life, is he dead—well, re-dead—now, too? How does this magic work?"

"There could be two killers," Dusi said. "The one who killed Burgess, and now the one who killed Marlene."

"I suppose." But my gut said that was too coincidental.

"Do you think..." Dusi started, then pressed her lips together.

"No, go ahead and ask. No bad ideas here."

"Burgess. Do you think he hated his sister enough to kill her? The invisibility spell would give him all the cover he needed to get away with it."

"That's smart. A really good angle."

"But?" she asked.

"I just don't think he would ever lower himself to physical violence. He was all bluster and bologna and put himself above others so they would serve him. He's manipulative and egotistical but doesn't want to lift a finger. I don't think he could hate anyone enough to actually do them harm. He'd rather make other people do it for him."

"I knew people like that." She put the car in park. "They made delightful statues."

"Dusi!" I laughed.

She just grinned.

"Thank you for driving me home," I said. "You're not going to walk to your place, are you?"

"No, I'm coming in with you."

I loved having visitors. I went out of my way to be social and to find people to spend time with, people to help.

But I was miserable that I'd read the whole situation so wrong. Marlene hadn't been the killer. She'd just been old and angry.

In the end, she'd become a victim. Possibly a victim of the person who'd killed and raised Burgess from the dead.

I had wanted to stop the killer, but I'd been as useful as a frog in a tug of war.

"I think I just want to be alone," I said. "Well, after Delaney comes over and asks me all the questions I've already answered, again."

She frowned, and the snakes under her scarf hissed in disapproval. "How about I stay until Delaney leaves? Jules, let me make you some cocoa and keep you company. Let someone do something nice for *you* for a change."

She looked so hopeful, I couldn't say no.

"As long as you're not expecting me to be a sparkling conversationalist," I warned.

She smiled. "I'll sit with you in silence if you want."

"Well, let's not go that far." I blew out a breath, surprised at how emotional I felt. "Okay. So. Cocoa?"

"On it."

We got out of the car, Tufa hopping along ahead of us. I opened the door and we all wiped our feet and went in. Dusi glided over to the tea counter and made herself busy. Tufa waddled to the couch and disappeared beneath it.

Soft sounds and music from the shop let me know Marty was still working. It was strange to realize the normal world carried on, despite shocks or tragedies.

I walked out into the shop to check in with him.

Mrs. Swider was thumbing through the incense, sniffing each pack and stacking some to one side. A tourist in tie-dye held a crystal in each palm, his eyes closed.

Marty sat on a stool behind the counter, reading a book.

"Hey, Jules." He lowered the book and walked toward me. "Are you okay? I heard."

"How did you hear?"

"Piper called to make sure I could cover a longer shift."

Piper. I suppose that was one benefit of having a friend who could see possible futures. She could help handle the details when the present got shaky.

"Do you want to lie down maybe? I can close tonight."

Wow. How bad did I look?

"I am fine." At his expression, I pulled my shoulders back and tipped up my chin. "I am. It was just unexpected and sad. You can go home if you want, I'll close."

"You know I have nowhere else to be. How about I stay? I've got a good book to read."

"You're not going to go no matter what I say, are you?"

"Nope."

"Stubborn."

"Yep."

"Too much of your mother in you."

He grinned. "Oh, just the right amount."

"If Delaney comes through, send her on back, okay?"

"You got it."

I straightened a couple crystals on the shelf that didn't need straightening, then walked back to the extra room and flopped into the softest chair.

"I'm hanging up my hat."

Dusi turned. "For what?"

"Mysteries. The vampire can have the stupid compact mirror."

"Mmmm."

"I don't know why I thought I could find a killer. I can't even find the guy who turned himself invisible with a spell *I* made." I accepted the cup she offered and took a sip. Deep, rich, just the right amount of sweetness.

"Oh. This is *good* good. If you ever get tired of art, you should become a chocolatier."

"We already have a candy maker in the family." She sat across from me, kicked off her shoes, and tucked her legs beneath her. "Don't tell her I stole her secrets."

I held my cup up in a toast and took another sip.

"Delaney and her sisters are good at keeping Ordinary safe," she said. "They're good at upholding the laws for supernaturals and everyone else."

"I know. They don't need me meddling in their business."

She hummed again. "I was going to say, they have a lot on their plates. Ordinary is...a lot.

"Helping if you can, especially when there is a killer in town, especially when your magic has been stolen? Tracking down clues or leads when it's a part of your past and your present? That isn't a bad thing."

"Well, it hasn't been a good thing, either. It's been a nothing thing."

"Don't hang up your hat yet."

"I was so sure Marlene had to have been the one who dug up Burgess. I was sure she was angry enough to kill him. But no. I got everything wrong."

She was quiet for a long moment, then she pulled off her mirrored glasses.

She was careful to look over my shoulder, and a bit high, so there was no chance she would turn me to stone, but she'd never taken her glasses off in front of me before.

I held very still. Her eyes were beautiful—mesmerizing green and gold, with flecks of ocean gray.

"Jules." Her voice was still soft, still patient, but those eyes gave each word so much more impact.

"You can give up on this if you want. Yes. But do not do it because you think you are a failure, or that you are less than what you hope to be. Failure isn't an ending. It is just a sign to begin again."

Someone knocked on the back door.

"Hey," Delaney called out, "it's me."

Dusi dropped her glasses in place and waved me to stay where I was. She opened the door and Delaney stepped in, her pet baby pig (that I was pretty sure was a dragon in disguise) trotting at her heels.

"Hi," Delaney said to Dusi. "I just wanted to ask again, how are you doing?"

Dusi seemed surprised she would ask, but Delaney genuinely cared about all of us here in this ridiculous town. It showed in the way she listened, in the way she fairly carried out the rules and laws, and in the careful way she showed her respect.

"I'm well," Dusi said after a moment's hesitation. "Would you give me a ride home after this?"

I didn't realize how down Delaney had looked until she brightened at those words. "I'd be happy to."

The pig snuffled Dusi's feet then turned to stare at the space under the couch. Those beady eyes flickered with flame (like I said—dragon) and it stomped my way. It stopped next to my chair and oinked.

"What?" I asked.

It oinked again.

"Sorry, I don't speak pig. Or dragon."

The eyes narrowed. It lifted a hoof and tapped my foot. Then it oinked again, but this time the oink was a lot more growl, a sound a pig should not be able to make.

"Food? Drink? Tarot reading?" I asked.

It bumped its little head into my ankle and stayed there like I was the dumbest witch in the West.

I reached down, my bracelets jangling and scratched behind its ears. It rumbled happily, and I chuckled. "You like that, huh? Who's a sweet piggy? You're a sweet piggy."

Tufa rocketed out from under the couch and tackled the pig, scrambling to stay on its back, and losing hold. He tumbled onto the floor and raced back to hide under the couch.

The pig just stood there stoically. It snorted, and warm smoke covered my feet. Then it turned and started toward the couch.

"No eating the golem," Delaney warned. "No chewing, chomping, or being mean. Got it?"

The little pig grunted and somehow made it sound like a rude suggestion.

Delaney pointed. "You can wait outside instead."

The piggy sighed and sat next to the couch. It oinked and tipped its head to one side, making one ear flop.

Delaney shook her head. "Nope. No negotiation."

Tufa belly crawled out from beneath the couch, stretching his paw toward the pig's tail.

"I wouldn't," Dusi said.

Tufa took a swipe at the tail. That pig spun and pounced faster than any natural animal could.

Tufa took off at a run, hiding behind Dusi's legs. The pig stomped his way.

Dusi scooped up the otter and rubbed his little head. "I told you, Tufa. Don't pick fights you can't win."

Tufa yawned, entirely unrepentant.

The knot of sadness in my chest (probably mostly self-pity) eased and my shoulders relaxed.

Things might not be good right now, but not everything was bad, either.

Also, it made me realize how much I missed having a pet. They were comforting, always got into shenanigans, and kept life interesting. I wondered if I should get one.

Delaney pulled up a chair and sat. "All right, Auntie. Let's go over it all again. Tell me everything you know."

I sighed and started from the top.

CHAPTER 12

Friday morning came on sunny and clear, but not warm because this was March in Oregon, and warm didn't show up until June.

The shop was open, and sunlight shining through the crystals hanging in the windows sent rainbows swimming across shelves and walls.

I flipped Tarot cards onto the counter in front of me, looking for clues in the images.

"Where are you, Burgess?" I muttered. "That spell should have worn off by now. Where have you gone?"

The Tarot was no help. Eight of swords, four of pentacles, five of swords—all cards of not moving forward, holding on too tightly, not letting go, and not knowing which battles to choose.

Either the cards were telling me to get over myself and move forward past this whole mystery business, or they were saying Burgess was stuck, and wherever he was, he wasn't making any quick moves.

"Okay, be that way. Let's try a bit of magic, then." I placed the cards back in their silk bag.

I took a deep breath and called on magic, drawing the pretty colored threads of it from my shop, from the stones, the wood, water, and music. I drew the magic pooled deep within my Fool Moon token buried beneath the door jamb and held it in my breath and in my hands.

"Call to me if you need help, Burgess Carmichael. I will hear you." I wove my words and voice into the flow of magic, casting the spell out through the air, out past my shop, out into Ordinary.

Burgess had answered that kind of spell before. If he wanted to, I expected him to answer it again.

Over the next few hours, only three people wandered into the shop, and two of them wanted directions to the Puffin Muffin.

Sunny weather always drew more tourists toward the beach.

With the Ladle-to-Grave beginning tonight at 9:00, I'd need to close the shop for a couple hours to get ready. I wanted to make sure the displays were in good shape, and that the outside could accommodate small crowds. Maybe I'd get in a nap before the night really took off.

No time like the present. I turned the sign to CLOSED and got to work on the displays.

Clara had blamed West for Burgess's murder. West had left his Tarot reading in a rush that almost looked like panic when I'd told him someone was betraying him.

Maybe West was more of a suspect than I thought.

"Did you do it, West? Did you kill Burgess and come back to town to take something from him? If so, why did you need to raise him from the dead? Why not just rob his grave, steal the item and cover it all up?

"Or are you the murderer, Clara? If so, same questions.

"Who else? Who am I missing? There are plenty of magic people in town. How many of them had a grudge against my old teacher?"

I snorted. "Anyone who met him, I bet."

The chime rang and the shop door opened.

I'd forgotten to lock it. "We're closed."

"The door's unlocked," Rossi said.

I turned from the blank journal shelf and pointed. "Sign says CLOSED."

"It does. And this side of it says OPEN. I'm going to take that as an invitation and just let myself in."

I huffed a laugh. "All right. Are you here to shop before the crowds show up?"

"Not exactly." He strolled over to the counter and leaned his elbow on it, his thin body canted sideways. If he was trying to look casual, he couldn't have chosen a more awkward way to do it.

"A little batty told me we might have a murder in town."

"Sage?"

He tapped his nose. "Frankly, I'd forgotten Marlene lived in that old house."

"We all did."

"The murderer didn't."

"I know. You don't happen to know anyone who hates taxidermized birds do you?"

"In general or in specific?"

"Either."

"No."

I laughed. "You are no help, Rossi."

"Well, you're the one who said you could solve the next murder before Delaney. How's that going?"

"Who said I'm trying to solve it?"

He gave me a look.

"Fine. It couldn't be going worse, thank you."

"Well, it hasn't been that long. You're following up on clues and suspects and," he wiggled his fingers, "all that detective stuff?"

"Clues going nowhere. Not enough suspects, and they all look innocent."

"Looks, my dear, are deceiving. Those who seem most innocent almost always have something to hide. Who do you least suspect at the moment?"

"Marlene. Since she's dead."

He grinned. "All right. Second-to-least suspect?"

"I don't want to say."

"That sounds interesting." He waited like he had years to waste. And since he was immortal, he did.

"Fine. Clara."

"Clara?"

"A witch I knew—know. A witch I hate. I want her to be guilty, but she's less likely to be the suspect than another witch I know. And...well, I used to like him just fine. It's confusing."

"How can it be confusing when you only have two suspects?"

"Because the other one who I thought did it just died. Which reminds me. Where were you last night, Rossi?"

That earned me a smile with a flash of fang. "I promised you I wouldn't commit murder to tip the scales of our bet." He leaned toward me. "I was at home. You can ask anyone in my family. We were playing board games."

"Lots of people are playing board games lately, aren't they? Marty thinks he could set up a board game café and people would use it."

"I would," he said. "Especially if it was open at night. Even more if it provided *interesting* refreshments."

I grunted and pulled my phone out of my pocket to make a note to tell Marty that, but my phone was dead.

"Do you want my advice?" he asked, as I stuffed my phone back in my pocket.

"No."

"My advice is that you should think it through logically."

"Wow."

"What?"

"That's it? Your advice is: Don't follow your heart?"

"I'm just saying none of the great detectives in literature let their hearts get in the way."

"What kind of literature are you reading? You're

telling me not to use my intuition? Hunches are every-thing for detectives."

"I didn't say don't use your intuition, I said don't let your *heart*—your feelings, Jules, good or bad—get in the way of looking at the situation clearly."

"Uh-huh. Is that advice to help me solve the crime, in which case you lose the bet, or are you hoping I'll bungle the investigation, in which case you win the bet?"

"What does your heart say?"

I laughed. "It says you're just trying to make it worse. Good-bye, Rossi. The shop is closed."

He cackled and pushed off the counter. "I'm just trying to be helpful."

"Sure, you are." I waved him out of the place, ignoring his entreaties for me to believe he was really and honestly just trying to be supportive.

Rossi might be annoying, but the conversation helped me make up my mind.

I needed to talk to West and Clara again. One of them had to be the killer. I just needed to keep my meddling heart out of it.

The shop was in good shape for the festival, inside and out, which meant I had time to go find one of them and ask some more questions.

Clara had been more than happy to rat out West. Maybe with a little extra prodding she'd go into more detail as to why she thought he had killed Burgess. Or she might know if he had a grudge against Marlene.

Or if he hated taxidermized birds.

I drove to Clara's house and marched down the straight sidewalk between fences to her front door.

I knocked.

It took a minute before the door finally opened.

"Jules?" Clara looked...well, she looked surprised, but also...pale? Her white-blonde hair seemed to have gone lank, and dark circles were smeared under her eyes. Even her lips appeared bloodless.

She looked like she hadn't slept in a week. If it weren't for her dress—a perfect pale yellow with layers of fluff that made it look expensive—I'd have guessed she'd just rolled out of bed with the worst flu ever.

"What's wrong?" I asked without thinking.

She looked up and down the street, then grabbed my sleeve and dragged me into the house.

There were no lights on in the place, but enough ambient light filtered through the windows to see by. Still, the whole house gave me the feeling she wanted it to look empty, abandoned.

"Have you seen West?" she asked.

I put my hand over her ice-cold fingers. She swallowed and released her grip on me.

"I saw him...I guess it was day before yesterday," I said. "Why?"

"He's so angry." She paced to the pile of clothes on the couch, picked up a fist full of them and threw them into an open suitcase on the floor.

"He came by. Right here, at my house. He accused *me* of betraying him. Of luring him out here to make an offer to buy my house. He accused me of digging up Burgess and pinning it on him. Do I look like I could dig up a grave?" Her voice rose as she talked.

"I think he wants to kill me." She flapped a pair of red underwear like a flag in a high wind. "Maybe you, too, Jules! He's...he's not the same. You see it. You see that, don't you? How he's different? He's scheming, acting all nice. But he wants us dead. All of us. Dead."

I had seen a lot of people during moments of trauma. Being a witch and a Tarot reader meant I'd seen people when they were struggling, spiraling.

Clara was obviously spiraling, probably because she hadn't slept or was sick. And, well, the murders had done a job on her nerves, too.

"Clara." I pulled the panties out of her cold hand and placed them on top of the messy suitcase. "Let's go sit in the kitchen and have some tea. We can talk. Have you slept?"

"No? I mean, I don't think so? What day is it?"

"Yup, it's time for tea." I steered her into the kitchen, which was white on white on white and far too modern for this old house. I sat her at the table and made myself busy opening cupboards, looking for tea.

"He was here," she said quietly, all the fire out of her. "I told him to leave. He didn't want to leave."

"But he left? Eventually?"

She nodded.

"That's good. You know you could always call Delaney—the police—and she or her sisters would come and help you." I chose a soothing mint and chamomile, dropped the bag in the cup, and filled it with the in-sink heated water tap.

I handed her the cup.

"I can handle him," she said with a little more pep. "I can do a lot of things on my own, Jules."

For a moment, she was the old Clara I knew. The one who wanted power, who wanted to be the best of us, better than all of us. The Clara who would do anything to get her way, and to wield power and cruelty over others.

She took a sip of the tea and made a disgusted face. "Terrible tea. No taste at all."

I ignored her. "You told me West killed Burgess."

"Did I?"

"You did."

"He *hated* Burgess. Burgess preyed on his ambitions and played him for a fool. Burgess just wanted him for his token. Wanted all of us for our tokens. And now West wants that, too!

"It's the tokens, Jules! West is killing for them!" She pulled her wrist with the charm bracelet closer to her chest, her eyes wide. "You and I should hide ours. Hide them together. Are you wearing yours?"

"No, it's at my shop," I said in a calming tone. "It's fine. Really, it's fine. But if you want to hide yours or maybe put it in a safety deposit box, I can help you with that."

She shook her head, her eyes more pupil than they should have been, boring into me. "No. He's going to kill us. He's going to take our tokens, then he'll do a spell.

The spell. I'm leaving. I'm almost packed, then I'll be gone. He'll never find me. Or my token."

"All right," I said, wanting to keep her talking to find out if she had any proof behind all that emotion. "Can you tell me how you know he's going to do this? What clued you in?"

For a moment, it was like I'd traveled back in time and we were classmates again. She drew herself up, the contempt on her face tight and mean.

"Don't play dumb, Juley," she scolded. "After all these years, you think I'd fall for that? You know the tokens are a gateway to immortality. Burgess told us. He even showed me how it was done. West wants to live forever, the self-centered so-and-so. He dumped you, remember? I thought I could change him. Make a life with him. But then he dumped me too, 'to find himself.'"

And yes, she did the finger-quote thing.

"Once he kills us all, he'll raise us from the dead—just like he did to Burgess—and he'll use our tokens to become immortal, and we'll all *die!*"

She stood and was around the table so fast, it was like she wasn't even human.

"You need to go. Now. Out. I have to pack. Good-bye, Juley. I never liked you."

I am not a small woman, but she pushed me to the door with supernatural strength. That was twice now she'd been able to physically push me around. I didn't like it.

But she locked the door, and skittered away toward

the back of the house where she couldn't be seen through the windows before I could say anything.

"You are *so* weird," I sighed, lingering on the doorstep. "And you were no help at all."

I turned and a light near the bottom of the house caught my eye. The basement window was behind a flowerbed full of rhodies and heather bushes. I took a step toward it, curious, but then the light winked out, leaving the entire house dark.

CHAPTER 13

Cake was the answer to my mood. Or at least it had never failed to cheer me up before.

I strolled into the Puffin Muffin and ordered some kind of dark chocolate sour cream wonder and a cup of strong black tea. I took both over to the same little table where Dusi, Piper, and I had sat yesterday.

The shop had been done up in black streamers with silver sparkly moons and cupcakes hanging from the windows. Hogan, the genius baker who was half Jinn and owned the shop, had lined the windows with strings of purple and pink lights, giving the whole place a spooky but cozy feel.

I still wasn't sure a Halloween-type celebration would work in March, but Bertie hadn't been wrong about any of the other wacky town events she'd put on.

The orange and purple lights strewn from light post to light post down the main street looked amazing. All around town huge silver moons swayed in every partici-pating shop's window or over its front step.

Ordinary had taken on a whole new vibe.

A vibe that suited me fine.

Was I moping about Clara insisting the killer was West, who I certainly should not have feelings for?

A little.

But more than that, I was disappointed my latest spell hadn't found Burgess, and Marlene had been murdered and, well, the extra whipped cream Hogan had added to the cake was appreciated.

I got through half the slice before my brain really started picking apart what Clara had said.

Marlene and Burgess and West all suspected each other to be the killer, but none of them (well, except for Marlene) had thought I might be the killer.

Why not? I was a witch. I was in the class with them. Didn't I seem like the killing type?

I mean, the answer to that was no, but the way they'd just dismissed me made it seem like they had all stayed in contact with each other much longer than I had. They knew more dirt on each other and had strong, mostly angry, feelings toward each other.

If this really was about needing all the tokens and raising the dead for immortality, then there could be another suspect.

Maybe Burgess himself was behind it all. He loved turning us against each other. He loved shifting the blame.

He said he hated necromancy, but he was a self-centered, egotistical liar. He might have raised himself from the dead and killed Marlene to get her token. Maybe that was why he hadn't contacted me—he wanted to remain invisible. It was the perfect cover for a murderer.

On the other hand, if Clara was right (and yeah, I wished she wasn't), then West could already have Burgess and Marlene's tokens, and of course his own. He only needed Clara's and mine to complete the immortality spell.

"And to kill us," I mumbled over the rim of my cup. "Unless Clara is full of nonsense and there's another more practical reason why Marlene and Burgess were killed. I mean, that house has to be worth something."

The bell over the door rang, and I looked up.

West had paused in the doorway, one hand still on the handle, scanning the room, his gaze coming back to me again and again. He was trying to decide something. Trying to decide if he was going to talk to me or walk out while he had the chance.

Ridiculous. I waved and gestured at the empty chair at the table.

He seemed to take an extended moment to pull himself together, relaxing his shoulders, then sauntering over, arms loose.

"Hello, Jules." His deep voice sent chills down my arms. "May I join you?"

"Sure. Did you want coffee, or...?"

"No, I was just..." he pulled out the chair and sat, "looking for someone." He turned up the wattage on the smile, and I tried to decide if it reached his eyes. "And here you are."

It sounded like a cheesy pickup line. If I were younger, I might be flattered, or at least chuckle at it, but I wasn't feeling all that young at the moment.

"I was hoping to see you today, too," I said, all my past feelings right where they belonged—in the past.

Thank you, Rossi.

"Oh?"

"Have you heard Marlene is gone?"

He paused, fingers curling inward, almost but not quite a fist. "I wondered if something had happened. I saw the ambulance going up that way. She was a lot older than us, wasn't she?" His voice changed, softened. "But then, none of us are as young as we appear to be. You chose your twenties?"

"Thirties. It's vanity, I suppose," I said, trying to think of how to ask him if he was a killer. "You chose your fifties?"

"It feels more honest to who I am. Wrinkles and all."

"No, it looks good. Good on you."

"Mmmm," he said, folding his hands on the table. "Go on."

Nope. Time to get down to business.

"Clara, though, she looks like she's eighteen," I said.

He frowned and no longer seemed as relaxed.

"Yeah. It's a little extreme," he admitted.

"She told me she thought someone might have been looking for Marlene's token. That someone is looking for all of our tokens," I said.

He knitted his brows, looked out the window, then back to me. "I hate to admit I thought the same thing," he said smoothly. "I even confronted her about it. Went to her place." He winced.

"That tarot reading…it made me think maybe she was going to betray me. I came out here with the idea of buying her house. But maybe she just wanted my token? All our tokens?"

"You think *she's* the one who wants them?" I asked.

"I know she does. She's asked for mine, multiple times." His hand shifted unconsciously to the leather and metal cord around his neck. I couldn't see it beneath his button-down shirt, but I assumed his token was there.

"She's asked me if I knew where you kept yours, too," he hinted, as if I'd just come out and tell him.

"How would you know where my token is? We haven't seen each other in years." I laughed, but it was a little forced.

"I know. But who else would even know Marlene had a token? How many people know how powerful the tokens are? Or that they even exist? Clara…she's…paranoid, I think. And she's still obsessed with that class. With those years we all spent together.

"She's never moved past it. Never grown beyond the idea that she was the most special witch. She never stopped trying to be Burgess's rightful heir. I've heard her say those exact words. His rightful heir.

"Plus she obviously wants to stay young," he went on. "Maybe she's finally realized that she isn't as young as she looks. That she isn't immortal."

He spread his hands flat on the table. They looked like hands that had done work, created things, *lived*.

Were they the hands of a killer?

I sipped tea, giving myself a moment to think.

Clara did seem like the kind of person who peaked in high school.

West appeared in his fifties.

I liked that. I liked that he wasn't trying to hide the experience of his life. Wasn't trying to pretend he was fresh out of college.

I always thought of myself as the same. I might look younger, but I wasn't trying to hide the life I'd lived.

"Listen," he said, "I want to apologize. I've thought about coming to see you so many times over the years, but like a jerk, I chickened out. I know I treated you badly, leaving so suddenly. I kept the truth from you, too. I want to come clean now."

Heat prickled my cheeks. "You don't need to drag up old mistakes. I've moved on. Let's forget about it."

"I can't forget about it. Let me...please let me apologize."

He looked so earnest. He was sweating, tense, like this was costing him.

"All right."

He opened his hands. "I apologize for breaking up with you. I never stopped caring for you. Never stopped...loving you. But I didn't want you tangled in things I wasn't even sure I could handle. I was wrong about that, too." He sat back and shook his head. "I never handled anything. I ran from everything. You deserved the truth from me then. If you want, I'll tell it to you now."

I'd just said that I didn't need to hear old mistakes, but sue me. I was curious. "Go ahead."

He scratched at his beard. "It was Clara. She told me she loved me, and hated you, pretty much simultaneously. I told her I didn't care what she thought about you and me. But then she talked me into letting her show me the private lessons she'd been getting from Burgess. You know all those long nights they used to spend together?"

I nodded.

"He was teaching her necromancy."

The sounds of the bakery—soft Brit pop playing on the speakers, the hum of an oven working in the back, the low conversations and clink of cups on wooden tabletops—all seemed to fade, replaced by a high ringing in my ears.

"He couldn't have," I said. "He hates necromancy. He told me so."

"He told you? When?"

"Just..." I caught myself before saying more. "He refused to teach it to us. And that spell, you know, the immortality one? He never taught us that, either."

"Jules, I'm telling you he taught it to Clara. She was very proud he chose her for that power. She wanted me to join her and Burgess back then to get all our tokens and start the spell."

Something was wrong with my face. It felt numb. "You all got together back then and tried it without me?"

"No. I said no. Marlene did, too when she found out.

She was furious with her brother and didn't want anything to do with Clara or him. I thought if I left the group, if I left everyone…"

"…even me."

"…even you, that it would stop Clara and Burgess from trying to cast the spell. They needed our tokens. It was easy to keep mine far away from everyone."

"You couldn't have just buried your token? Hidden it?"

He blew out a breath and looked at the ceiling. "I didn't want to give up the magic in it." He looked back down at me. "I chose my magic over everything. Over you. Over us."

"And you left."

"I left. Traveled. Saw the world. I made so many more bad decisions." He once again interlocked his fingers on the table.

"I wanted to find you, but I was ashamed of how I'd left. I'd given up the best relationship I'd ever had, the most wonderful woman I'd ever met, because I was afraid of what Burgess and Clara wanted to do with my magic.

"It was selfish. I'm sorry, Jules, for leaving you. I'm sorry for giving up on us, giving up on you. I'm sorry I was afraid. And impulsive. And so very *shallow*. I'm sorry it's taken me so many years to have the guts to tell you this."

I couldn't deal with his remorse, couldn't really accept it might be real. Not until I knew the truth.

"Did you dig up Burgess and kill Marlene?" I asked.

His eyes went wide. "What—how do you—"

"Jules!" Marty pushed through the door. I hadn't seen panic on my nephew's face since that day he'd thought he'd accidentally eaten three toads. Yes, three. Accidentally.

"You need to come to the shop. Now." He scowled at West and picked up my empty cup and plate, putting them in the little return cart by the counter. "Hurry."

"What's wrong?" I was on my feet, following him out the door. "Are you okay? Is everybody all right? Was there a fire?"

"There was a break-in," he said. "Someone tore the shop apart."

CHAPTER 14

Broken shelves, ripped books, tables tipped over, crystals scattered everywhere. The shop was a disaster.

"They were looking for something," I said. I think I'd said it a half dozen times, but I couldn't seem to say anything else.

"Do you have any idea what that might be?" Delaney asked gently.

Piper had (of course) rolled up just as Marty and I had gotten to the store. She'd righted a chair for me and put a soft lap blanket over my legs.

I told her I didn't need it, but the blanket was warm, and weirdly, I was shivering.

"They broke the lock," I said. "They got into my shop. *My* shop."

"You have it warded with magic, don't you?" Delaney asked.

"Yes. That's—how would someone break in without me knowing?"

"Or me," Piper said grimly. "I should have...I should have seen something. But I didn't. Nothing."

"They must have used magic," Delaney said. "Or some other kind of power. Neither of you are to blame in this. Jules, can you tell how they broke the ward?"

"Yes, I think...I should be able to tell." I didn't know why I hadn't looked for that in the first place.

I stood, waving away her offer to help, and strode to the door. I whispered a spell and opened myself to the magic of the broken ward. Magic lifted, crackling up from the floor and swirling out of the walls. It zipped to my fingertips and curled up to my ears, telling me the tale.

"A witch broke in here," I said. "They used a spell I've never seen. It's like a mix of a dozen spells."

"Can you tell who it was? Which witch?" Delaney had that intense look, almost as if starlight was reflecting in the blue of her eyes.

She carried Ordinary's power and the magic this gods-blessed land carried. Her family had been chosen with the responsibility of upholding the law and caring for all who lived here. It wasn't a small thing to be in charge of a place where gods vacationed as mortals, and other magical people like me, could live undetected in peace.

She was ready to use every power Ordinary gave her to find who broke into my shop, my home.

"The magic is a...mixture of spells that don't make sense. I don't recognize it."

"Are you sure?" Piper asked. "It's probably West or Clara, right? They're both in town, they're witches, and they treated you terribly in the past. Maybe they wanted to mess up your shop. Steal your token."

"What token?" Delaney asked.

I filled her in on all the weird token stuff Clara and West had talked about.

"Auntie, you should have told me about the tokens," she said.

"I just found out when they got back to town. And there's no proof West or Clara are telling the truth about the immortality spell or the tokens."

"You don't think it was West or Clara who broke the ward?" she asked.

"I don't know. I don't think it's West—or at least it's not like magic he used to cast. But it doesn't feel like Clara's magic either. This is...muddled. Twisted." I shook my fingers and let go of the shop's magic. "I know that doesn't help."

"It's okay," Delaney said. "Knowing it's a witch gives me something to go on. I'll find West and Clara and talk to them. Don't worry about this, Jules. I'll take care of it. Don't try to find who did it, either. That's my job.

"Your job," she continued, "is to decide if you want to reopen the shop for the festival kick-off in a couple hours. I can talk to Bertie if you want to stay closed."

"I promised her I'd be a first stop on the map."

"She will understand. Bertie doesn't always have to get her way."

We both just stared at each other, silence spreading between us because well, that just wasn't true.

"She really does though," I said.

Delaney snorted. "Well, she can find another way to get her way, then."

I chuckled. "I'm not going to be the one to tell her that. I can still be a first stop on the map. I'll just put the hot drinks outside and close the shop. I think I can get it in shape by in time to open tomorrow."

Delaney frowned. "Let me help. I've got a few minutes."

"No, it's okay. I've got this." Then, to head off the argument I knew she'd give me: "I'll miss one night of the festival. That will only make the shop more popular tomorrow. I'm fine, everyone is fine, no one is hurt, and you have a lot on your plate. Have you gotten any leads on where Burgess might be?"

"Nothing useful, which is really annoying. I don't think he left Ordinary, but I haven't found a single shred of evidence he's still here. Has the invisibility spell worn off, do you think?"

"It should have, but I really did mix up a strong one, so maybe not. Again, I'm not very helpful."

"Now, none of that. This isn't your fault. Even if you hadn't cast that spell and found Burgess by his grave, someone would have found him. Things might have been the same as they are, or worse." She glanced around the shop. "Are you sure I can't help clean?"

A knock on the door made Piper grin. "Not necessary. We'll get it fixed up in no time!" She opened the door.

Sage strode in, Fawn behind her. They both had brooms and buckets of cleaning supplies.

"Hey, Jules," Sage said.

"Front of the shop first?" Fawn pointed.

"Um..." I said.

"Yes," Piper said. "Good idea."

Than strolled across the threshold next. He held a box of pink garbage bags that smelled like lilac. "For refuse." He nodded at Delaney. "Reed Daughter."

"Just Delaney," she said. "You skipping your shift?"

"I will be at my station at the required time."

"Take as long as you need. We can cover."

Xtelle—in her human form—pushed her way in. She wore an outfit that was, in my opinion as a person who wore a lot of sparkles, a little over the top. Did anyone need that many feathers or a golden scaled top that left her stomach bare but scooped up like an umbrella over her head?

She glared at everyone and crossed her arms. "I refuse to lower myself to menial labor. Pan, Avnas. Attend me."

Pan, the god, trotted up to her. He was a small white goat with magnificent golden curled horns. "Yes, my love," he said. "Here, my love."

Powering in right behind him was a muscular miniature black bull. Avnas was a demon who had been the right-hand man to the king of hell—but who was now hanging out in Ordinary, dating Xtelle. Or maybe dating

Pan. Or both of them. I couldn't keep track of their relationship status.

Avnas rolled his eyes and snapped his hoof, turning into his human form.

He had been a warrior, and it showed. Silver hair, square jaw, lines across his forehead. Even though he wore a black T-shirt and slacks, he emanated the power of someone who had spent a few millennia leading battles.

"I will assess the area," he declared, "and rally the troops." He strode through the room, rugged, ready, and ridiculous.

"So powerful," Xtelle murmured.

Pan made a raspberry sound. "As if he ever cleaned up after a party in his life. I, however, am a deft hand at restoring beauty from chaos. I'll show you." He trotted after Avnas, throwing, "Hi, Delaney," over his shoulder.

"Hey, Pan," she replied.

"Wait," I said. "You don't have to do this."

Neither Pan nor Avnas paid any attention to me.

Herman (troll) and Lochlan (bluecap) walked in, one with a mop, and one with a stack of pizzas.

"Got the call," Lochlan said. "Should I put the pizzas in the back?"

"Really, I can get it all sorted," I said.

"The back is best," Piper said. "Perfect."

"Where do you want me to mop?" Herman asked.

I opened my mouth to argue, but Piper just touched my arm. "I called in the book club. Everyone except Ottilie and Delta were able to come help. Let them help."

Herman nodded. "Happy to lend a hand. Us G.O.O.B.eR.s gotta stick together." He chuckled at our club's acronym, and I couldn't help it, I chuckled too.

"We really went for it with that name, didn't we?" I said.

"I like it," he said. "Keeps us from taking life, and all those horse-based books, too seriously."

"I heard that!" Xtelle shouted from the back.

Herman grinned. "Where do you want the mop?"

Piper sent him into the back and told him to work his way toward the front.

Dusi tapped on the door and let herself in. She scanned the room, then walked over to me. "I'm sorry." She opened her arms.

I was surprised to feel tears trickling down my cheeks as I accepted her hug. "It's okay. I'm angry my wards didn't hold. I'm angry someone could mess with my life, mess with my things."

"We'll fix it," she said quietly. "We'll find out who did this, and then we'll fix them, too."

I huffed a laugh and gave her an extra squeeze in thanks, then let her go.

"The gang's all here—well most of us," I said. "You can head out, Delaney. I'll let you know if I need anything."

"Promise you will," she warned.

I crossed my fingers. "Promise."

She gave me a look. "That's not how it works, Auntie."

"It does when you're a witch." I winked.

"You always say that when you want to break the rules."

"Shush. Witchery is mysterious."

She smiled and paused at the door. "Are you really okay?"

"I am." I gestured at Piper and Dusi, and everyone else laughing, working, and on the part of Lochland, singing slightly off key. "I really am."

"Don't forget to reset your wards."

"I couldn't possibly."

She closed the door, and I turned to Piper and Dusi. "I talked to West again."

"Talk," Piper said. "This is going to be good. I mean, I think it's going to be good?"

"He found me at the Puffin Muffin. He wanted to apologize. For our past."

"For everything in your past?" Dusi asked.

"Just for the stupid choices he made. He said he regrets choosing magic over me. Regrets leaving me."

Piper made a happy sound, but Dusi narrowed her eyes. "Did you ask him if he killed Burgess?"

"I asked him if he dug him up and killed Marlene."

"And?" Dusi leaned in.

"That's when Marty rushed in to tell you what happened here," Piper said. "I mean, right? Marty showed up?"

I nodded. "Yes. West didn't answer me, but he looked shocked that I'd asked. I think...I don't want to think this, but he might have done it. I could see him hating Burgess and Clara and Marlene enough to have done something about it."

Saying that out loud made my heart drop. But like Rossi had said, I needed to keep my heart out of this.

I swallowed, determined to see it through. The truth was the truth. Ignoring it, or hoping for something different, wouldn't change that.

Sometimes a person we once loved turns out to not be who we thought they were. Sometimes we have to face that head on.

"Why him?" Dusi asked. "Why do you think West might have killed Burgess?"

"Clara's a liar, but she's not wrong. West hated Burgess just as much as I did. Marlene hated him, too. Only Clara liked him, or maybe it was that he liked her. And West...he's angry. Even if he's trying to hide it."

"Angry enough to kill a man?" Piper asked.

I remembered West's hands, warm against my skin. His laugh that always cut out halfway only to come roaring back. I remembered the promises he would whisper against my temple as he held me tight.

My heart wanted to say no, but I wasn't listening to it anymore.

"People change. I know I have since back in those days. But West? Once he makes a decision, he sees it through. Even if it's a bad decision."

"Did you tell Delaney you think he did it?" Dusi asked.

"I told her it might be either of them, which it still could be. I told her about the tokens, too."

There was a crash from the back room, and Xtelle giggled. Someone, likely Than, said something that cut her laugh short.

"Now." I stood. "I've decided I'm done solving the murders. That's Delaney's job. It's time for me to do mine, which is looking after my shop, and looking after the people who are going to stop in tonight."

"Jules," Piper said. "I don't think you should quit. That's uh...*sight* talking."

I gave her a smile. "Sight or no sight, right now, I just want to clean. There's a festival coming up, and I'm not going to let a little mess stop me from being a part of it."

She and Dusi both gave me a hug, then rolled up their sleeves and began putting the shop back together again. Not for the first time, I was so happy for the friends in my life.

Q

I WAS SURPRISED HOW QUICKLY THE SHOP WAS CLEANED. I EVEN had enough time to make a quick sandwich for dinner before the first festival attendee strolled in, wide-eyed and excited.

We'd strategically rearranged the merchandise and lowered the lights, relying on the display lights and lots of electric candles to give the shop a mysterious feel.

Marty had draped pretty gold scarves in the windows and set up a small fan to blow on a little chime.

I knew Bertie pulled out all the stops for every event,

but I'd wondered how much foot traffic could be drummed up on a cold, rainy March night.

Turned out I never should have doubted her. I sold dozens of crystals, sage smudge sticks, incense, Tarot, scarves, journals, books, fountains, beads, necklaces, and even one large carved elephant.

The hot drinks went over swimmingly, and people lingered both inside and outside. I didn't know how it started, but as the night went on, more people wore glow bands, light up necklaces, and LED hats. One person had an entire vest that flashed pixelated video game characters.

But the last graveyard tour had left twenty minutes ago.

"Not bad," Marty said around a yawn. It was half past midnight, and except for the folks still enjoying food and drinks in the restaurants and bars, the festival was over for the night. "Good start for a Friday. It's going to be really rolling tomorrow. Need me to help you pull some stock?"

"Absolutely not. You've done enough today. Go home, get some sleep. I'll tackle getting new stuff out in the morning—late morning."

"Okay, then." He rambled over and gave me a huge hug. "You get some sleep."

"I will."

"Auntie."

I laughed and gave him a shove. "I will. Go."

He left, pointing at the new lock on the door before he closed it.

I took a deep breath, then walked slowly through the shop, touching all my grounding points, checking with the magic infused in the space.

My token was still beneath the threshold, but I was curious to see if it had been messed with in any way. I knelt in front of the door and released the spells keeping the token buried there. It only took a moment with a screwdriver to remove the wood threshold.

I picked up the small silk bag and pulled out the token. It flashed silver, hanging from the leather string braided with a silver chain woven through it. Only West made those kinds of chains, and this was a gift from him I'd never been able to let go of.

My token, just like the others, most resembled a coin. Carved on one side was the fool, one foot over a cliff, a rose in her hand, bindle on her shoulder, and cat at her feet. On the other side was a simple carving of the moon.

Magic radiated from the token, singing out and echoed by the rest of the shop, as if a soft wind had suddenly been called upon to bring ease and rest.

I looped the chain around my neck, the weight of chain and token against my skin both familiar and strange. I replaced the threshold, shut and locked the door, and walked the interior of my shop again. Then I walked all of my home, resetting the magic, powering the wards, and setting magic free to embrace the small space I called my own.

What I should do is go to bed. But I was still restless, the emotional load of the day too heavy. I wanted some fresh air.

I wandered outside. It was dark, and the nearly full moon hovered low over the ocean. The night was quiet now, all the lights off in the shops, the excitement of the festival hushed.

I wandered to the edge of the sidewalk, turned, and considered my shop. Nothing seemed different about it. There was no indication it had been disturbed or broken into. I had spells in place that discouraged people from leaving litter or stomping on the plants and flowers.

It was good to do the rounds, though, and after several minutes the cool air had cleared my head and lowered my shoulders.

Did I really think West killed Burgess? I blew out a breath and stared up at the stars. My heart still said no, but when it came to him, my heart had never been right.

Someone had killed our mentor years ago. Someone had raised him from the dead.

Someone had killed Marlene. And while Marlene's death appeared to be an attack, no one except Clara had suspected Burgess had been murdered.

Why would the same killer kill so many years apart? Were they desperate, reckless? Were they running out of time?

"Did you do it, West?" I whispered to the stars. "Were you so angry with the past that you were willing to ruin your future?"

The stars said nothing in return.

Halfway back to the shop, I noticed a glitter of light on the ground. Something had fallen in the bushes.

"Come on," I huffed. "I know my anti-litter spell isn't broken."

I reached between the rhododendron's broad flat leaves and pulled out a string.

No, not a string. A very familiar length of braided leather with a thin gold chain woven through it. The kind of chain that only West made. The chain that held his token. He'd been wearing it this evening.

It was broken—cut clean through. Whoever had cut it knew they'd have to get through leather and metal.

The clasp was still intact, but the token was missing.

Everything in me went on high alert. West had been here, standing around outside in the crowd? Was he Spying? Stalking? Waiting for his turn for a graveyard tour?

Or had he been jumped?

If he'd been jumped, was it the murderer? Or did someone else cut his chain?

"Slow down, slow down," I said. "I don't know that he was jumped."

But what was the other option? That West had cut the chain himself and thrown it in my bushes?

If not that, then who could have snuck up on him? Who could have overpowered him?

Maybe an invisible Burgess?

If the killer wasn't West, then the only other people who knew the tokens were powerful were me, Clara, and Burgess.

I didn't know where Burgess might be, hadn't once thought to ask where West was staying. But there was one way to cross Clara off the list. She'd said she was leaving town. It was a short drive to her house. Easy to see if she was still there or if the place was empty and locked up tight.

I grabbed my keys, hopped in the car and headed out.

CHAPTER 15

This shouldn't be hard. Just get out of the car, walk up to the house, and snoop around a little. There were plenty of windows in the front I could peep through. If I could get through the bushes, I should be able to see into the basement windows, too.

Plus, there was a door in the back. If the front was locked, maybe the back would be open.

Loads of spying opportunities. I just had to get to the spying.

The FOR SALE sign staked in the middle of the yard rocked in the gusty wind. It felt like a warning, a reminder.

This house was no longer a home. This house had been hollowed out, emptied of people, of things, of purpose.

It was waiting to transform, waiting for whomever would turn it into a home, a business, a storage space.

But somehow the presence of Clara seemed to linger, haunting the place.

Empty houses didn't usually creep me out, but this one did.

"It's just an empty vacation rental," I told myself. "Lots of those in town. Why are you still in the car, Jules?"

I thought about calling someone. Piper, Dusi, heck, even Delaney. But it was so late it was almost early again. Night festivals were a challenge because everyone was trying to work both day shifts and night shifts to be sure to keep the tourists entertained and happy.

I should be home, in my nice warm bed. Not out here sleuthing when I'd promised I was all sleuthed out.

"You're a big girl, Jules," I said, making sure my keys and phone were in my coat pocket. "You're just going to see if Clara is home. And if she is, ask her if she's seen West. Easy."

I pushed out of the car, the wind whipping my hair away from my face and molding my skirt around my legs. If I hadn't known better, I'd have thought the wind was trying to push me away from the house.

It wasn't raining, but everything was damp from the heavy marine air. By the time I reached the house, I felt like over-spritzed grocery store lettuce.

The windows on either side of the porch were dark. I worked my way past the wet bushes and cupped my hand to look through the glass. My breath steamed the window, but even holding my breath didn't help me see inside.

I threw a tiny little spell to give my eyes the ability to pierce the darkness.

The room seemed bathed in a soft red light and came into sharp detail. Everything was the same as it had been before—very clean and impersonal.

I once again had the feeling the space was suspended, waiting to become something.

No light shone from the basement windows, and even though I bent to get a look, the glass was fogged, like someone had sprayed a thin layer of paint over them. I walked up the porch and tried the front door. Locked.

"The back it is, then."

West's chain was tucked in my pocket and my token was around my neck. The spell for sight in darkness would last a little longer, so it was easy to see my way.

The path along the side of the house was tangled with tall, dead grass from last summer that wrapped around my ankles and tightened, forcing me to tug free with each step.

It was almost as if everything was trying to stop me from getting closer to the house. I rounded the corner and the wind gusted hard enough I had to duck my head and plow forward.

The backyard was just as overgrown as the side yard. Clara needed a word with whomever was in charge of mowing. The front was immaculate, but the back, which couldn't be seen from the road, was a mess.

I made it to the back door and tried the doorknob.

No, I did not expect it to open.

Yes, I had to slap my hand over my mouth to muffle my squeal of joy when it did.

I did a little happy dance, then calmed myself and stepped in without a second thought. I shut the door behind me and took a moment to slow my breathing.

The house was silent and dark, shadows deepened from the sight spell I'd cast.

I'd stepped into a mud room that connected to the kitchen. I could see straight through to the living room. It seemed twice as large as I remembered, the chemical pine scent from cleaning agents filling the air.

It was so silent I could hear the echo of my heartbeat.

"Clara?" I whispered.

The wind battered at the roof.

"Are you here?"

No response. I walked through the kitchen and studied the living room. The suitcase and clothes were gone, everything clean and static.

Maybe she'd left and forgotten to lock the back door.

To my left was a closed door, and a very faint light leaked out from beneath it.

Was this the door to the basement Dusi had mentioned?

There was no other light coming from what I assumed were the open bedroom doors, but just to make sure, I crept to each and peeked in.

Nothing but bedroom furniture.

I tip-toed back to the basement door and placed my hand on the door handle. It turned, the small click sounding like the snap of a trigger.

I pushed the door open just a crack.

It felt like I waited forever, but there were no other sounds, no murderers jumping out of the shadows to murder me, no witches throwing around ward-breaking spells.

All I needed to do was check the basement, and then I'd know for sure that Clara was gone.

I pushed the door open a little more, slow and careful.

Just a basement, I thought.

Old wooden stairs curved downward, a worn wooden handrail bolted to one wall, disappearing into that faint light. From the cold damp smell, it hadn't been used in a while.

Nothing to do but go down there. See why the light had been left on.

I took one step onto the stair, just as a hand dropped onto my shoulder, gripping tight.

CHAPTER 16

I screamed.

Yeah, not my finest moment.

I am not a delicate woman, and I don't try to make myself quiet or timid. When I laugh, I laugh with my whole body.

And when I scream...well, if the neighbors weren't awake before, they were now.

"Be quiet!" a voice sputtered.

I spun on my heel (holding the handrail because I was not about to be shoved down the stairs).

There was no one there.

"What are you doing here?" a man's voice asked out of empty air.

I recognized that voice.

"Burgess?"

"I said to keep your voice down."

I refocused on the air in front of me. He had to be there, invisible. His words weren't coming from a speaker, they were coming from the space directly in front of me.

"You're *still* invisible?" I said in a slightly lower volume.

"You forget that I am a witch and more than capable of changing, enhancing, and modifying spells on my own. Why, I taught the basics of that invisibility spell in the first month of classes you took from me. It's witching 101."

"No, it's not," I said. "You didn't. My spells..." I cut off. The last thing I needed right now was to argue with the invisible man I'd been looking for.

Plus, I'd found him first before Delaney. Take that, Rossi.

"Have you been in this house the whole time?"

"No. Not that it's any of your business. I've been reading."

"What?"

"The book? Oh, do keep up, Ms. Larkwood. I told you I had been reading a book before I was interrupted by my own murder. And so I've read it. I don't believe it was all a dream. That girl really did travel to OZ and kill that poor witch."

"You've been hiding out in the library this whole time?"

"It's called unfinished business, Ms. Larkwood. There is virtue in completing one's tasks."

I wanted to yell in frustration, but I took a breath and kept my voice low. "Why are you *here*?"

"To confront my killer, who I am nearly positive isn't

you. Not because you might not want to kill me but because you have zero follow through.”

“What?”

“Always late with your assignments. Too many days staring at butterflies and shiny objects and too many nights staring at Mr. Heath, I assume.”

“Excuse me? I could be the killer if I wanted to be. I turned in one spell late. *One*. And that was because you sent me to organize your library—which was a mess—and you wanted it done by the end of the day.”

“You were also late to organize my library, proving my point.”

It was good he wasn’t visible because I’d have kicked him in the ankle.

“You hacked my invisibility spell to make it last longer,” I hissed.

The silence was telling. Hacking another witch’s spell was highly frowned upon, and Burgess gave us no end of grief if we even peeked at each other’s work.

“I modified and improved it,” he said.

“Which is against the rules.”

“Whose rules?”

“Yours!”

“Bah. Witches have been…improvising for centuries.”

“You said it was strictly forbidden!”

“Is that why you killed me?”

“I didn’t kill you, you old blowhard. I wasn’t even in Ordinary back then.”

“Obviously,” he said, refusing to admit he was wrong. “West is my killer.”

"West?"

"West."

"Why do you think he did it? You told me you didn't remember who attacked you."

"I don't remember. But he was the worst student, well, besides you. He was angry I wouldn't let him learn the immortality spell. He wanted that spell enough he left you. Clara told me he tried to convince Clara to teach it to him. When she didn't—because she, at least, was loyal to me—he must have decided to kill me. And now he dug me up, stole my token, and left me undead."

"Someone stole your token?" I asked, picking up on that detail.

"Yes. I am certain it would have been buried with me. I had specifically written it in my will."

All the doubts came flooding back. He sounded so certain it was West.

But I had evidence in my hand—the broken chain—that someone had taken West's token.

Unless West had planted that broken chain as a trap and wanted to lure me out to Clara's house to trap me in the basement.

"I'd wager West wanted to lure you out to Clara's house and trap you in the basement," Burgess said. "And here you are, falling right into his hands because you could never think logically when it came to him."

"You're wrong." The words were quiet, but strong enough I could feel the heat of anger warming my face. "I might have been in love with him, but I never slacked on my schooling, and I never put my relationship above my responsibilities. You have always thought the absolute worst of people. You love trying to make everyone think the worst of others and themselves and I've had enough of it.

"If West is the killer, then fine." I had to swallow over the ashy lump in my throat. "Then fine," I repeated, "he's the killer. But until I confront him and ask him if he did it, I am not going to assume he did it just because a bully like you said so."

Since he was invisible, I had no idea what he thought about that.

The silence stretched for long enough it passed the awkward stage and just became annoying.

"Have you confronted West?" I asked.

"Of course not."

"Do you know where he is?"

I heard him inhale, then there was silence again. Just long enough I wondered if he had left, or if he was looking for an invisible weapon to knock me over the head with.

"I believe he is in the basement."

"Believe?"

"You don't expect me to go down there do you?"

"Of course not. You never do anything you can make someone else do for you."

"I beg your pardon. I was waiting for the police to arrive."

"Oh good, you called the police," I said, surprised he had done something useful.

"With what phone, Ms. Larkwood? You will call them."

"Really over you trying to boss me around, Burgess. I'm not your student anymore."

"Obviously."

I pulled out my phone. It was dead. I took a deep breath and stuffed it back into my pocket.

"I'll call after we see if West or Clara are here."

A shuffling sound from below made me jump—no scream this time, yay me—and grip the railing even harder. That could have been an animal.

Or a murderer.

"Well?" Burgess stage-whispered. "What are you waiting for?"

I pressed my free hand over the token resting on my chest, drawing on the comfort of that magic, tied to my shop, my life, my happiest place.

Then I turned and started down the stairs.

With every step the space became darker, colder. It smelled of wet concrete and dust, still but not stagnant air.

The house hadn't been lived in full time for several years, but cleaners must have come through the basement now and then because there was a broom leaning against one of the walls near the top of the stairs.

Still, it felt like I was slowly descending into an impenetrable darkness, the tread uneven beneath each downward step, my palm sweating and sticking to the rail each time I lifted and dropped it.

My throat seemed full of dust, and I wanted to clear

it, but the silence grew unbreakable, dangerous, so I just swallowed and swallowed.

I ducked near the lower half of the stairs. The main floor was mostly above me but slightly blocked my view of the room below.

The stairs took a hard right turn at the bottom, which was obviously an afterthought because they were too short and uneven in height.

I had to pay close attention to where I put my feet or end up breaking an ankle.

When I reached the bottom, the movement right in front of me made me jump again.

"Juley," Clara said, so close I could smell something like mold wafting off her clothes. She was ghastly pale, far too bloodless against the dim light, her eyes ringed with shadow, as if she hadn't slept in years. "You are late to the party."

She lifted a gun and pointed it at my face.

CHAPTER 17

M agic is fast, but bullets are faster. I think I'd read that in a book somewhere.

Still, magic was not a thing to underestimate. I wiggled my fingers and called on the magic stored in my token.

Nothing happened.

No response to my call. No magic available to me. At all. It had been blocked so completely, my ears hurt from the pressure of feeling no magic around me.

Clara bared her teeth in a semblance of a smile. "You can't use your magic here, Juley. I've cut it off and locked this place down. I was *dying* to see that look on your face!" Her laugh was shrill and frantic. "Move." She ticked the gun slightly to one side. "That way."

My thoughts ping-ponged between outrage and panic. She had a gun (a *gun!*) and I'd blithely walked into the basement thinking my magic would keep me safe.

She'd blocked *all* my magic.

Why hadn't I brought a weapon—I mean, not a gun because I didn't own one, but a knife could have helped. Or a working phone.

I walked as slowly as I could, my eyes finally adjusted to the darkness.

The basement stored random furniture against the walls, tables, chairs, and what looked like a spare set of washer and dryer. The small windows near the ceiling were painted over. A single, yellowed lightbulb in the middle of the bare rafter ceiling cast the only light.

But what demanded my immediate attention was the circle and pentagram drawn onto the concrete floor, and the five chairs around it set at each point of the pentagram.

Two of those chairs were occupied.

"Marlene? West?" My voice was loud, shock and fear peppered with anger.

Neither of them responded. Marlene was slumped to one side, and I was pretty sure she wasn't breathing— which made sense, because she was dead.

West, in the chair next to her, was bound by ropes that radiated Clara's winter cold magic. His eyes were open, unblinking, and his mouth was gagged. He held supernaturally still.

Frozen.

He didn't look as pale and dead as Burgess or Marlene—or come to think of it, Clara—but he did look older, closer to his actual age.

I thought I saw his chest rise and fall.

Please let him be breathing, I thought. *Please let him be alive.*

His token glinted dully on the floor in front of his feet. Marlene's token was in front of her chair, too, and there was another token, maybe Clara's, in front of an empty chair.

That left two other empty chairs. It didn't take a genius to figure out one was for me, and one was for Burgess.

"What are you doing, Clara?" I asked, the panic losing ground to anger. I never could dwell on the enormity of a situation without wanting to jump straight toward solutions. "Did you steal Marlene from the morgue?"

She made a rude sound. "This town is too busy with its festivals to pay any attention to one missing dead body."

"So that's a yes. You know stealing dead people is a crime."

"Only if they catch me," she shot back. "Which they won't. So shut up and sit down."

Yeah, that was never happening. I needed to buy myself time to come up with a solution that wouldn't get me, or West, dead.

I didn't think Delaney was on her way, unless she had gotten up early and suddenly deduced Clara was the killer.

Piper could see the future, though. But I didn't know if she had clear sight on this situation. She'd been thrown off by the magic used to break the wards of my shop. There was a slim possibility she might know I needed help.

If she did, would she call Delaney or come over here herself?

No, I couldn't rely on her riding to my rescue. Marty, Dusi, and everyone else didn't know I was missing and wouldn't expect me to be awake for hours.

I was on my own here.

"You killed Burgess, didn't you?" I walked as slowly as possible across the space.

"Yes, of course I killed him! He was the first who had to fall. If the spell is to work, I had to take him out first."

"I thought you said you weren't strong enough to knock him out."

She scoffed. "Magic can make anyone strong, Juley. I even overpowered West."

"But it's been decades. What took you so long to undead Burgess? Don't tell me it took you that long to learn necromancy. I thought you were his best student."

"I am. I just didn't get around to it until now. Until I realized that time...never mind."

But it hit me.

Clara was still trying to look like a teenager. She wanted to look young, to be young. Now that she had hit her seventies, she must have realized that no matter how young her magic made her look, time was still rushing forward. Someday she'd simply run out of time.

"You want to be immortal. You...you think you're running out of time, out of chances to work the magic. Because none of us are getting any younger and if one of us dies and you can't dig us up, or find our token, you're stuck being mortal."

"The only thing I'm running out of time for is killing every one of you and raising you back to life by the light of the full moon."

"It was Marlene," I said. "You saw she was putting the Rookery up for sale. You were worried she would… What? Die before you got a chance to kill her? So, you came here, lured West here on the pretense of selling your house to him and dug up Burgess's grave."

"Look at that. Even a C average student can get the answer right once in a while. Keep moving." She twitched the gun again.

"But you didn't know if bringing Burgess back to life had worked. Or maybe you did? How did you get him out of the grave?"

"You think I can't throw an undetectable levitation spell? Please."

"Then why just leave him out there on the dirt?"

"It was…going to rain and I hate the rain."

"No." I said, the pieces falling into place. "You couldn't find his token. You thought it was in his grave, and cast the spell, but he didn't wake up right away, did he?"

"It's this stupid town. I have to hide everything I do from its stupid magic. I'll find that token. I will. I can feel it. As soon as you tell me where you put Burgess, I'll make that old idiot tell me where he hid it."

"You don't know where Burgess is?"

"I *did*. But he's *invisible*. I had to kidnap West and

steal Marlene and break your stupid wards. I just don't know where he is *now*."

She didn't know he was in the house.

Maybe I could use that to my advantage.

"He must have hidden his token in Ordinary," I said. "But you already tore apart the Rookery looking for it, didn't you?"

"Marlene and her stupid stuffed birds. I thought he'd hidden it in one of those. But there was nothing. Nothing!" She stomped her foot, which looked weird on a woman holding a gun. "But now I have West and I have you. I just need to find Burgess before the full moon is over. Sit down so I can tie you up. I only have a few hours left."

"Then what?"

"Then I'll kill you and West, bring you back to life, and one-two-three I'll be immortal and you will all be wrong. Just like I always knew you were."

"How?"

"What?"

"How are you going to kill us? With a gun? You know this is a small town, right? Your neighbors are going to hear it. There are still people out there walking around after the Ladle-to-Grave. The police will be here so fast, you won't have any time to cast a spell, much less do something as complicated as reanimating us and casting an immortality spell."

She rolled her eyes and reached into the cute little bag hanging from her shoulder. She pulled out a metal fitting of some sort. "Silencer," she said. "Did you really think I wouldn't think this through? I'm the smart one, remember?"

"Well, you're not smarter than Burgess."

"What?"

"I said you aren't smarter than Burgess!"

"Why are you yelling?" she yelled.

"Because I want to make this clear. You really think Burgess is dumb?"

She took a big breath and then got into it with her whole chest. "Burgess has always been an old, doddering fool who is too dumb to know his ideas about magic are outdated, weak, and wrong. I could beat him at any magical form or spell. He smells bad, has terrible taste, and I lied to him for years. 'Oh, you're so smart.' 'Yes, mentor Carmichael, you're perfect.' 'You're so powerful and I'm just an innocent little witch who needs your help.'

"I *never* needed his help. I needed access to his library so I could steal the necromancy books he had locked away."

"*You're* the one who tore his library apart," I said. "I thought you liked him."

"I hated him. No, wait." She tipped her head. "I *pitied* him, the old self-righteous windbag. Too dumb to know all of us were laughing at him behind his back."

"I never laughed—"

"Shut up!" She still had enough air to really make that crack across the rafters. "You are going to give me your token, and you are going to sit in that chair. Now."

She thumbed off the gun's safety. From the look in her eyes, she was hoping I'd give her a reason to shoot.

I was very aware of how bad the situation was. This woman would be more than happy to kill me because she needed me dead to become immortal.

Logic told me to sit in the chair. Logic told me to get away from that gun—or to do anything to make her put it down.

But my instincts said if I sat in that chair, I was already dead.

I held up my hands. "Clara, let me help you work this out. I'll tell you where Burgess is. I'll help you tap the magic in my token—in all of our tokens. It has to be a big job. Let me help you with it."

"The only way you can help me is if you're dead. And, you know, brought back to life by me," she added. "Sit down so I can kill you."

Well, this was it then.

"No."

I refused to let her boss me around. Even with a gun pointed straight at my chest and West probably in danger behind me, I would not passively do what she said. I just hoped that when she brought me back to life I'd remember that I hated her and would somehow foul up her spell.

"I don't need you sitting to kill you, Juley." Her finger twitched.

"Then you'll never find Burgess," I said.

"I am not a self-righteous windbag, you nit!" a voice bellowed.

Burgess was running—well, lumbering—across the room, the invisibility spell stripped away as he crossed into the no-magic zone Clara had cast.

Clara turned. She wasn't slow, but the sight of our old teacher, pale, undead, his flesh saggier than ever, wearing my sparkly skirt, Christmas leggings, and seagull hat, while brandishing a broom in one hand, must have caught her by surprise.

Surprise that lasted only a split second.

She lifted the gun and fired.

CHAPTER 18

"No!" I yelled.

But Burgess had gathered too much steam to be stopped by a bullet. He rammed forward and collided with Clara, the broom flying out of his hand and clattering across the floor.

Clara got off another shot.

I rushed in, drawing on my magic in an automatic knee-jerk reaction.

I cast a powerful spell to freeze them both in place.

Except my magic didn't work. Clara had smothered all magic in the basement.

Okay. Fine.

My magic wasn't the only magic in the world. Ordinary carried its own power, given to it by gods, goddesses, and other supernatural beings.

I'd promised Delaney I wouldn't do big spell work in town.

I'd promised Delaney I wouldn't call on Ordinary's powerful magic.

But this was a matter of life and death. Promises were going to be broken and I would apologize if I got out of this alive.

I stretched out for Ordinary's magic, calling it from the rocks, the soil, the streams. I reached for Ordinary's magic in the roots, the trees, the ocean crashing against the shore and in the sky, clouds, stars and moon.

Ordinary's magic heard my call and woke, a huge, powerful beast made of sand and sea, blood and bone, leaf and limb. It roared, ringing like a massive bell in the distance that grew louder, and louder.

Coming toward me like a locomotive.

By the time I reached Clara and Burgess who were wrestling for the gun on the floor, that great bell tolled once, tolled twice, tolled thrice...

...and broke over me with a tsunami of magic.

It triggered the last spell I'd cast, crackling with fire. Beautiful arcs of blues, purples, reds and oranges folded around both of them like a blanket that wrapped and squeezed.

Of course, my spell wasn't the only spell in the room. There was also Clara's pentagram on the floor that would power her immortality spell.

More magic flared, silver sparkles snapping tiny fireworks through the air, gold melting and flowing down the walls like waterfalls of liquid metal that crashed across the floor and filled the pentagram with light.

West made a sound, but I couldn't spare him a

glance. There was still a gun and two very angry witches on the floor.

I snapped my fingers, casting light, and the room was instantly daylight bright.

"Where is the gun?" I demanded. "Who has the gun? Are you hurt? Are both of you hurt?"

I spotted the gun to the left of Burgess and Clara then hustled to pick it up. My hands were sweating as I put the safety on, then cast a second spell to ensure it would stay in my purse and wouldn't discharge.

West made another sound.

"What?" I asked turning.

He strained against the ropes, talking around his gag.

"Hold on, hold on," I said.

I checked the witches on the floor one more time.

They were certainly frozen. My spell had carried a heck of a punch.

They were identically pale, the shadows on their faces bruised and dark, rings around their eyes almost raccoonish.

Clara looked even worse than Burgess, her hair lank and messy and gray, deep wrinkles across her forehead, around her eyes, and her mouth. She looked her age, but more than that she looked bitter and mean.

They'd landed on their sides, with Burgess's back toward Clara's front—making Clara the big spoon— both of them reaching toward something.

I followed where their gazes were locked.

West? They were looking toward West?

The pentagram on the floor pulsed with golden light flowing toward...Marlene.

Marlene jolted upright, her eyes wide, her skin dead-woman-white.

"What in the fowlfeathers is going on?" she yelled.

West strained harder against his ropes, and Marlene who had been dead just a minute ago, stood up.

"What?" she repeated, brushing awkwardly at the gold magic covering her.

"Who cast this? Ugh. Clara. Is this your spell? Ick. It's everywhere. I told you when you came looking for his token that I'd never tell you..."

That was when she noticed she was in a basement, by a pentagram that was channeling a necromancy spell, the very spell that had just turned her—like her brother—into an undead.

"Oh, for pelican's sake! Really? You were so angry you didn't get your way you decided to kill *and* resurrect us? Why would I want to come back to the living? I was perfectly happy dead.

"You—" She stabbed a finger toward me. "Are you a part of this dark magic plan, too? I knew you were trouble."

"No! I'm trying to stop her," I pointed at Clara. "I found Burgess, and I'm saving West." I pointed at each in turn. "You all," I circled my finger in the air, "are making my life difficult during a festival when I haven't gotten any sleep and I would appreciate it if you would all stop it."

Marlene narrowed her eyes, West choked, but it

sounded like a laugh. Burgess and Clara—well, they were still frozen so they didn't say anything.

I stomped over to the pentagram and pulled off my token, placing it in the center of the spell.

Ordinary's magic filled my token and twinkly lights danced around the room. Twinkly lights that could absorb stray magic.

Clara's janky necromancy spell never had a chance against my magic, blended with Ordinary's. Her spell short-circuited and fizzled.

"Finally," I sighed. "Now, Marlene, please sit down."

"I didn't kill anyone," she said.

"I know."

She sniffed and sat in her chair.

I walked around the pentagram to behind West, then untied his hands and feet.

He pulled his arms forward, and I could tell he'd been there awhile because his movements were stiff. He reached up and pulled the gag out of his mouth. "Are you okay?" he asked, his voice hoarse.

"I'm fine. Stay here while I finish dealing with the two on the floor."

I strode back around the pentagram and stood over Clara and Burgess. "I'm going to release this spell. You are both going to wait for Delaney to get here. If you so much as twitch the wrong way, I'll wrap you back up and you'll stay frozen like that for a month. Understand?"

They didn't nod—because they couldn't—but there was something in their eyes that said they agreed.

I raised my hand and took a second to consider what

would happen if they didn't obey. There was a lot of magic filling the room. Could they use it against me?

"West," I asked, "Do you have your phone?"

"Yes, hang on, yes." He got up and walked over to me, still a little unsteady. Whatever spell Clara had used to keep him still must have been a whopper.

There were definitely more wrinkles on his face, and gray in his hair. Silver, actually. I liked it.

"Who are you calling?" He offered me the phone, and I took it without looking away from the witches on the floor.

"Delaney. Are you okay?"

He let out a breath. "I think so. That spell hit hard. I'm still getting my land legs."

I dialed 911 and was relieved to hear a familiar voice.

"Ordinary Police, this is Delaney Reed, what is your emergency?"

"Hey, honey. It's Jules. I found Burgess. And I found his killer. Oh, and you might be missing a body since Marlene's here, too. When you get a minute—no rush, I know it's early—could you come on over?"

"You...what? Jules, are you okay? Do not go into wherever that's happening. Wait for backup. I can be there in a second."

"So about that..."

She groaned. "You already went in, didn't you. Are you hurt?" Her tone was all business now.

"I am fine. Uninjured. I have everything under control. Just come over to Clara's vacation house. We're in the basement."

"Already on my way," she said. "Stay on the line with me."

"That's smart!" I said. "I wouldn't have thought of that. You've really gotten good at this job, kiddo."

"Jules," she said, and this time I could hear the power in her voice. "I need you to be very careful right now. Keep me on the line."

"You got it." I put her on speaker and set the phone on the washing machine. "All right, here we go, people. I'm going to release you from the stasis spell and you're going to promise to sit quietly and wait for Delaney to show up."

"Wait," West said.

"No!" Delaney said at the same time. "If they are secure, just leave them that way until I get there."

"But they're shot. I think. Maybe one of them."

"Shot?" Delaney demanded. "You did not tell me there was a firearm involved."

"There's no blood," West said, pitching his voice to reach the phone.

I glanced at him. He stood next to me, hands on his hips, steady and strong, looking down at Clara and Burgess with an intensity that did things to me.

But he was also standing like his back hurt a little. The lines on his face showed the years he'd lived, all of it visible and out in the open, instead of behind the magic he'd been using to make himself look younger.

"Can you unlock just enough of the spell so they can talk?" he asked.

"That's a pretty high level of witchery."

He lifted his gaze. "You're the best of us, Jules." His voice was soft and encouraging. "Always have been. I know you can do it."

It was startling to hear those words from him. All these years I'd thought he—all of them—had thought I was the weakest among them. I wasn't sure I agreed I was the best, but he wasn't wrong. I could handle complicated spell work.

"All right. Let's see what I can do."

I centered myself, feet to earth, mind to sky, heart and breath to spirit and soul.

I pulled Ordinary's magic to me again, softer this time, letting it ease into my heart, my words, into my desires and intentions.

I wiggled my fingers, working to carefully undo just enough of the binding spell around them to release their mouths.

"Did it work?" West asked.

"She did it!" Burgess bellowed.

"Oh, shut up!" Clara said.

"She killed me, she dug me up, she wanted my token, *and* she shot me!"

"No, you shot me!" she yelled. "And you don't even know where your token is."

"How dare you."

"I told you!" Marlene said. "I said I put it in a bird, but you wouldn't believe me. Then you tore up all *my* birds and killed me!"

"Marlene," Burgess scolded, "you were firmly

instructed to bury my token with me, not stuff it in a bird."

"I did both, you ungrateful lout. It's in your hat. Your seagull hat."

Burgess' eyes went wide, then something that looked like respect crossed his face. "Oh well done, Marlee. Well done."

The hat in question was in the corner, and I walked over, picked it up, and tucked it under my arm.

"Wait," I said, "you're both shot?"

"Well, I think I must be," Burgess said. "Even she couldn't have missed at such close range."

"I never liked you at any range!" she yelled.

"Then why aren't either of you bleeding?" West asked.

"Because they're both dead," I said. "Same pale faces, same dark circles, same, um...creepy zombie look."

"Hey!" Burgess and Clara said at once.

"Rude," Marlene added.

"The only thing I can't figure out is who brought *you* back to life, Clara? You brought Burgess back to life. We just saw you using Marlene's token to bring Marlene back to life. It couldn't have been Burgess because he said he was reading this whole time."

"Ha!" Clara said. "Fat lot you know."

"Burgess? You brought her to life? For the love of... you told me you hate necromancy."

"In my defense," Burgess said, "I did have questions. I demanded she answer them to my satisfaction. She had to be made undead to answer them."

"Wait," West asked. "Who killed Clara? Did Marlene do it?"

Clara made a rude sound. "I killed myself, you idiot. I wouldn't trust any of you to do it right."

"Do keep up, Mr. Heath," Burgess said. "Even Ms. Larkwood had that figured out."

"Yes," Clara grumped, "special little Juley figured it all out. Now you can unbind us. We've been shot, Juley, we've both been shot. I promise we'll be good until Delaney gets here."

"Maybe I can ease the spell so we can take a look at your wounds..."

West reached over and gently took my hand.

It startled me, I think it startled him, too. But when I glanced at him, he gave me the smile that made him look like he was twenty again and ready to get into any kind of trouble I could name.

"Maybe we just leave them there until the police come," he suggested.

"I...uh..." I said falling into the pull of his joy, the very magnetic, unconscious attractive energy of him that had caught my breath the first time I'd ever seen him.

"Yes!" Delaney said sternly over the speaker phone. "Wait for me to get there. I'm right outside."

I heard a car door slam, and footsteps—rushed and loud—as she stormed down the stairs, her sister, Jean right behind her.

"All right, everyone," Delaney said, taking in the scene and visibly relaxing when she saw me. "Let's get you all somewhere more comfortable so we can talk this out. Jean?"

"Got it," Jean, the youngest of the Reed sisters had on her uniform shirt today, which meant she had pulled either the overnight or the early shift. Her hair was purple and clipped back from her face with star and moon barrettes.

She gave me a smile, noticed West and I holding hands, and grinned even bigger and waggled her eyebrows. Then she strode over to Marlene.

"Hi there, Marlene," she said, helping the old gal stand. "You're looking a lot less dead than the last time I saw you."

"I want to register a complaint," Marlene said. "Against this town. A dead person has the right to stay dead, but oh no, not in Ordinary."

"Sure," Jean said. "We can get you a representative. Make sure your dissatisfaction with the town is registered."

Delaney stopped next to me and gave West a hard look. "Are you sure you're okay?"

"I am," I said, feeling those words resonate in a way they hadn't in a long time. "I really am."

She touched my shoulder, gave West one last look, and got to work arresting a couple of undead witches.

CHAPTER 19

"So, it was all about the immortality." Piper handed me a crystal in a green silk bag.

"Clara?" I said. "Yes. She wanted immortality and didn't care how many people she had to kill and bring back to life to get it. Including herself." I put the crystal on the table with the others, arranging them to catch the light from below the shelf to make them glow.

"Would it have worked?" Dusi adjusted the painting on the wall. It was a watercolor of my shop, and she'd somehow captured the joy, the magic, the love I'd always felt in it. "If she had killed you and West and brought you back to life, could she have attained immortality?"

I made a considering sound. "The necromancy spells were a little vague on the specific steps to immortality. Clara was making some pretty big guesses on how to fill the gaps. But she had spent years researching and modifying them."

"It might have worked," Dusi said.

"It might have. But it's more likely it would have just ended with us all being undead."

"Yeah," Piper said, digging into the delivery box for another stone. "I could see that. What did Delaney do with them?"

My shop door opened, the bell jingling.

"Speak of the angel. Hey, Delaney," I said.

"Hi. I thought I'd check in and see how you're doing."

"Me? Good. Just getting ready for the last night of festival. Want a cup of coffee?"

"I'm good, thanks." She glanced around the room. "I love how you've rearranged it. New art?"

"Dusi's letting me show some of her stuff."

"Jules is kindly letting me take space on her walls," Dusi replied.

"I love that. It's beautiful. Your art and her magic go so well together."

That earned a very rare small smile from Dusi. "Thank you."

"Everything okay?" I asked Delaney. "Do you need my help with something?"

"I just wanted to give you an update on Clara, Burgess, and Marlene."

I stopped fussing with the stone display, worry settling over me. "Are they still in jail?"

"Yes. They'll stay there until after the full moon and after the festival."

"What happens then?"

"None of them wanted to press charges for their murder."

"Oh," I said. "That's...unexpected."

"Clara did kill Burgess and Marlene though, right?" Piper asked.

"She confessed she did," Delaney said.

"I'm surprised Burgess doesn't want revenge," I said. "And I thought Marlene was ready to sue everyone in sight. Especially Clara for tearing her birds apart."

"They've had some time to talk it out and air their differences. Loudly. Marlene's not pressing charges for the destruction of her property. But that's not the only reason why I came by. Burgess wants to talk to you."

A cold chill rolled down my spine. The last thing I wanted was to ever talk to him again. He'd been a part of the past that I'd always wanted to keep in the past. The fact that he'd barged into my now hadn't changed my opinion.

"You want me to go to the magic jail?"

"No. Absolutely not. I have my phone. Jean, who is there right now, has hers. What do you think?"

"You don't have to," Dusi said.

I checked with Piper. She shrugged. "I don't think it will matter if you do or don't. Well, except for maybe satisfying your curiosity."

She was right. I was just curious enough to want to know what he had to say. "Let's go in the back. In case early customers show up."

"I'll watch the shop," Piper said.

Delaney and Dusi followed me to the back room. Delaney and I sat on the couch and Dusi made tea.

"Are you sure, Auntie? You don't have to do this."

"He lectured you about how he legally is allowed a phone call, didn't he?"

"At length. But still..."

"No, I'm fine. Let's do it."

She tapped her screen, waited for it to light up, then answered. "Delaney. Yep. Okay, I'm handing it over."

She offered her phone. I held it to my ear.

"Hello?" I said.

"Hey, Auntie," Jean said. "I'm putting my phone on speaker. Burgess wants to say something to you."

"Ok."

The sound of motion around the phone came through, and then Burgess cleared his throat. "Ms. Larkwood," he said. "I wanted to thank you for your assistance in the matters of my death."

My eyebrows shot up. "Assistance?"

"You did find me at the side of my grave, in the rain. And you gave me lodging, clothing, and an invisibility spell."

"You wrecked my house, took my clothes, and stole my invisibility spell."

"Yes, but had you not opened and operated that crowded little trinket shop of yours, Clara would not have thought she had a chance to get the five of us together again."

"Uh-huh. How is that a good thing?"

"I want you to know that while I hate Clara, her murdering and then resurrecting me did allow my sister and I to make amends."

"I hate Clara, too!" Marlene crowed in the background.

"Marlene and I will not press charges against Clara. We'd rather just leave this living world to its own devices, thank you very much."

I blinked. "What does that mean, Burgess?"

"Must I explain everything?" he groused. "Marlene and I will be leaving this earthly realm. Having had the chance to compare, we'd much rather have our eternal peace and quiet over the nonsense of this world."

"Oh." The mix of feelings was more than I could sort through, but relief was definitely one of them. "So, you're going to have someone kill you again?"

"A blunt way to say it, but yes. We will return to our comfortable slumber."

"I can't wait!" Marlene said. "It was so warm and cozy. And so many birds!"

"Congratulations?" I tried.

"Thank you. Also, we are leaving the Rookery in your name."

"What?"

"With one stipulation. You must, in some way, use it to be of service to the community."

"That was my idea!" Marlene said. "That house is historical, you know. People should appreciate how historical it is."

"Uh, I'd really rather you left it to someone else."

"No. We have left it to you. There. That's done. Good-bye, Ms. Larkwood. Enjoy your life."

The phone went quiet, then Jean said, "That's it, I think. Did you want to say anything else to them?"

"No, that was enough. Plenty."

Jean chuckled. "I'm glad you're okay, Auntie. Love you."

The call ended.

"Huh," I said pulling the phone away and staring at it. "So that's a thing."

"A bad thing?" Delaney asked.

"I have no idea. I don't suppose you want a big old drafty house up on the cliffs? It's historic."

"Ryder and I are happy in our house by the lake. What's that all about?"

"Burgess and Marlene gave me the Rookery."

Dusi made a surprised sound and handed me a cup of tea. The warmth of the cup between my hands was welcome.

"I didn't expect that," Dusi said.

"Neither did I. What am I going to do with it?"

"You could move there," Delaney said. "Fix it up."

"And leave my shop?"

"You could always take your shop with you," Dusi said.

"What?"

She pressed her lips together, considering. Then she nodded. "It has nice open sitting rooms on the main floor. You could set up your shop there. You could invite artists to show their work, maybe other craftspeople."

"You could rent out rooms to book clubs!" Piper suggested from the other room.

"And not Scrabble groups," Dusi agreed.

I laughed. "No Scrabble groups for sure."

"Do I want to know what that's about?" Delaney asked.

"No. It's just a petty feud. Xtelle's petty feud."

She groaned. "That woman is so much work."

Dusi laughed and pressed her fingers over her lips.

Delaney grinned at her. "You've met her, you know what I mean."

"We all know what you mean," I said. "Okay I'll think about what to do with the house. I'm not ready for a big challenge and that much change. Not yet."

"But I bet you will be," Delaney said. "That's what keeps life so interesting." She stood. "By the way? I love seeing you—the real you—more now."

"The hair?" I patted my hair which had more gray in it than brown, "or the wrinkles?" I laughed, still unsure if I was going to stay the way Clara's magic-stripping spell had left me.

It wasn't that I couldn't cast a new spell to make myself look whatever age I wanted to be, it was just that looking my age felt more freeing than I'd imagined.

"You," she said. "All of you. I like it. You look happy."

"I've always been happy."

She nodded. "Happier, I think."

"Well, I don't have to worry about a killer being loose in town."

"Now that you've won that bet with Rossi?"

"That snitch! He told you?"

"Yep," she grinned. "You let me know if he doesn't hold up his end of the deal."

"What's going to happen to Clara?" I asked.

"She's being charged with magical crimes, and mundane crimes, like murder. Even though she's undead, it doesn't mean she can escape the law. I have a feeling she'll be locked up for a long, long time, or for however long the raised-from-the-dead spell lasts."

I thought about Clara locked in a cell, with no fancy clothes, no fancy make-up, no token, and no one to pay attention to her and tell her she was the best witch.

Yeah, she was going to hate that.

The bell over my shop door jingled. I glanced at my watch. It was only nine o'clock, but people were already out shopping.

Bertie had once again managed to draw a massive crowd in for a festival I hadn't been sure would attract a dozen.

"Gotta hop." Delaney took a couple steps, then turned. "Oh. One more thing. I know you tapped into Ordinary's magic."

It was like the world stopped, all sound, all light dimming.

"I did," I said. "I know I broke my promise to you. I understand there are repercussions…"

"Auntie." She stood in front of me and dropped both hands on my arms. "It was life or death—your life or your death. I am so glad you used it." She pulled me into a hug and I exhaled.

"So, no repercussions?"

"No. I'm just glad you're safe. I love you."

I relaxed and squeezed her gently. "I love you, too, honey."

She leaned back. "But let's make sure this is the only time you have to do it. No more getting yourself into situations where you have to use big magic, okay?"

"You can count on it. I've had enough excitement for a lifetime, thank you."

She raised one eyebrow, obviously not believing me. "All right. Let me know if you need anything."

"I will." I wrapped her up in another quick hug then shooed her out of the shop.

Several tourists browsed the shelves, happily chatting about the stroll through the town, beach, and graveyard beneath the full moon yesterday.

Luckily, the rain had held off today, and it looked like it was going to be a clear March night again. A good last day of the festival.

"We have hot cocoa," I said to a woman who was rubbing her arms, "tea and coffee, too. Just help yourself."

She gave me a grateful look and headed for the beverage cart.

The rest of the day and night went by in a blur.

Just after midnight, the last graveyard tour had left, most of the shops had closed, and the trio of women who had bought a Tarot deck each were out the door with directions to Jump Off Jacks, which was keeping even later hours.

Marty said his good-byes, and was off to a late-night online gaming event.

I flipped the sign to CLOSED, turned on the twinkly lights, and took a deep breath.

The shop had been well-looked through, the displays were messy, the shelves picked and gleaned. It made me happy.

Plus, I'd booked readings for the next two months.

A knock on the door made me turn.

"Sorry," I called out. "We're closed."

"Jules," West said. "Do you have a moment?

West. Of all people.

My head told me not to open the door, but my heart, well...would it hurt to listen to it just this once?

West Heath stood there, bundled in a warm coat, a beanie on his head, and a question in the lift of his eyebrows.

He'd left my life years ago.

He'd broken my heart.

Years ago.

I was a different person now. Well, I was still the same, but I had more experience. I'd lived a lot of life. I knew what I wanted. I knew how to keep my heart safe.

But West had always been my Achilles heel.

"The shop's closed," I said again.

"I know." Clara's spell had drained our tokens and had done some damage to West's youth spell, too. He looked...well, he looked just as gorgeous as he ever did. The gray streaking his hair only made his eyes catch fire, and the wrinkles at his eyes and forehead showed proof of sorrow and laughter.

The full moon bathed him in a wealth of silver.

"Festival's over," I said.

He shifted his weight, not leaning closer but leaning just the same, a little, on the door frame. He nodded.

"I was thinking..." He pointed upward. "There's a full moon, not a cloud in the sky, and I still have a box of cookies from the Puffin Muffin."

"Impressive restraint, having any Puffin Muffin cookies left."

"I might have eaten one or two." He smiled, I smiled, and the silence of this strange time of night flowed between us like the soft pause of music between two songs.

"Why are you here, West?"

"To ask if you'd like to walk with me on the beach. To ask...." He looked down then up again. "I'm asking if you would like to spend some time with me. Because I would love to spend time with you. To get to know you again. Who you are now."

"This me? With the gray hair and saggy..." I waved my hands vaguely at my body, "and wrinkly fingers?"

He blinked, then shook his head. "This you, Jules. With your big laugh, and curious mind, and heart capable of caring for your family and friends and strangers in need. Rushing in to help, to rescue even when doing so might be hard, or dangerous. That's the you I've always seen. That's the you I've missed all these years."

It was my turn to be surprised.

He waited. I'd always liked that about him, his ability to wait and let a person—let me—feel my way through the moment.

Maybe it was the time of night. Half past midnight was made for questions and longings. Maybe it was the lingering magic of the full moon.

But my mind was clear and quiet, giving my heart room to decide.

"A walk sounds nice," I said. "Let me brew some tea to go with the cookies."

The smile he gave me outshone the stars.

CHAPTER 20

"It could use a deep clean," Piper said, kicking gently at feathers as she ducked under the crime tape.

"And light," Dusi added. "There isn't enough light in here." She'd tried to keep Tufa in the kangaroo bag, but the little otter had run off as soon as we'd walked into the Rookery.

We could hear where he was by the chitters, growls, and small crashes coming from the other rooms.

"But do you think we can do it?" I asked.

"We?" Dusi pulled the crime tape down and strolled into the main room.

"You didn't think I was going to move into this big old place and open it up as a community art center and market without you, did you? If you both think we can do it, we'll be partners in running the business side of things.

"Dusi, you'll have gallery space, of course, and there's plenty of room for a private studio, too, if you want.

Piper, I know you've been exploring designing knitwear. If you want..."

"Of course, I want to show my knitting! And maybe I could set up a yarn exchange. Oh, and give classes."

I laughed and she grinned.

Dusi did a slow circle. "How many rooms in this place?"

"I don't know. At least six on the main level. The upper level has a sitting room facing the ocean, four bedrooms and a kitchenette. There's an attic, too."

"It's going to take a lot of work," she murmured.

Piper strode to the windows and pulled back the heavy velvet curtains.

Soft afternoon light poured into the space.

"Lots of dust," I noted. "Historic dust."

"Good bones, though," Dusi said. "Historic bones."

"I like it," Piper announced. "We can do this, Jules. We can turn it into a gallery, a shop with a maker's market, and meeting spaces we could rent out. I think Bertie would be delighted to have a new event space. Plus, it's historic."

"Would you live here?" Dusi asked.

"I don't know. I think so. There's a...I guess it's a carriage house, or servant's quarters. It's a nice little cottage right behind the house connected by a covered walkway. It would be perfect."

"What would happen to your shop?" she asked.

"Marty is looking for a place to start a board game café. I could lease it to him."

"Oh, that's perfect!" Piper said.

"So, why not?" Dusi folded gracefully to sit on the arm of a couch. "Why not take this unexpected gift and make it into what you want?"

My hesitance was strange, even to me. What I had always wanted was a little shop of my own and a home of my own. A place where I could help my community, gather with my friends.

The Fool Moon had become that. I'd spent years making sure it had become that.

But if I were being honest with myself, I'd outgrown the space a long time ago.

With this building, I could have an entire room for Tarot readings or maybe lead meditation classes.

There could be a space to display art, a space for making art, a space for gathering. A space for the book club, no Scrabblers allowed.

And Dusi wasn't wrong. It did have good bones. For all that Marlene and Burgess had kept it closed up and hadn't updated it in fifty years, it was a sturdy old building. A little elbow grease would transform it into a beautiful, thriving space.

The only question was, did I want to be the one to do that?

"You can say no," Piper said quietly. "From what I can see…" She tipped her head, her eyes focused on futures I would never experience. "Not that it's much help, but from what I can see there isn't a bad choice here. You can be happy no matter where you are in your life, Jules. It's one of the things I love about you."

Dusi made a soft sound. "I agree."

Tufa galloped into the room, chittering and growling. Right behind him was a tiny white cat with gray tipped ears, tail, and foot.

"Kitty!" Piper said.

Tufa jumped up onto the couch, then hopped into Dusi's lap and spread out. He chittered down at the cat.

The kitten mewed, turned, and trotted straight over to me, settling on top of my foot. It mewed again, looking up at me.

"Aw." I bent and picked it—her, I thought—up.

She mewed one more time, then started purring, her little eyes closing as I pressed her against my chest. "Where did you come from?"

"I wonder if she was the cause of all that thumping upstairs we heard when we were first here with Marlene," Piper said. She walked over and petted the kitten's head. "Have you been here all alone, sweetheart?"

The kitten peeped a tiny half-meow, then went back to purring herself to sleep.

"Jules," Piper said, "I think you have a new friend."

"Aren't you an unexpected treat?" I murmured.

"Cats are good luck," Dusi said, which made Tufa growl in complaint. "Otters are chaotic luck." She scratched his little head and he chirped in agreement.

"So," Piper said. "How about it? Ready for maybe a couple of new changes in your life?"

I looked at the room around me, its possibilities, while holding the sweet little kitten and decided.

"Why not? But I don't want to do it alone. You both

need to take some time and think it over, too. Are you ready to get into business..."

"Yes!" Piper said.

"...hold on, and take on all the remodeling work..."

"Yes," Dusi said. She held up one finger. "I am extremely old enough to know my own mind, Jules. You are my friend. Both of you are. Let's go on this adventure together."

I laughed, loud and happy. "Then let's do it! To adventure!"

$$Q$$

"THIS IS IT!" I STRODE INTO THE SITTING ROOM, MY ARMS HELD wide. "Our very own meeting space. What do you think?"

It had been a week since the festival and all the dead/undead excitement with Burgess and Marlene and Clara.

Piper, Dusi, and I had had just enough time to sweep up the place, open windows, and do a light dusting.

The Rookery wasn't ready to open up for everyone yet—that would take months. But it was in good enough shape for our book club to meet.

Xtelle pussyfooted into the space, her pink horsey nose wrinkled up to show too many teeth. She had a gold cape tied around her neck and spread across her back, a monocle on one eye, and a tiny gold top hat between her ears.

"How...dull," she said. "Fine wood accents? Is this

linen wallpaper? And these furnishings, are they from the eighteen hundreds?"

"Yes," Piper said. "Isn't it beautiful?"

"I like it." Sage flopped down on the couch and stared up at the tin-tiled ceiling. "It has charm."

"Smells like bird," Fawn noted as she walked along the wall with the bookshelves stacked floor to ceiling. "But I like it, too. Lots more room than your shop."

"Or the library," Herman added.

Dusi leaned on the wall by the little area we'd set up for drinks and snacks. She'd hung one of her watercolors there, a beautiful scene of sunlight spearing through the forest to light a winding path.

It made me think of beginnings and new places to explore. I loved it and had spent several hours convincing her I wanted it as the first new piece of art in the new space.

"I think it's great," Delta (dryad) said, as she came back from peeking in the other rooms. "Perfect for our meetings, and a lot more."

Ottilie, who was a black cat shifter, had already curled up on the window seat where sunlight poured in. "Maybe a café?" she suggested.

"I'd like that," Lochlan said. "Books and snacks are my favorite."

Than strolled over to the bank of windows that looked out over the ocean. It was nice weather today, puffs of clouds sailing the blue sky, the ocean wrinkled green and gray velvet.

He locked his hands behind his back and was silent.

For some reason, everyone else in the room was silent, too, waiting on his judgement.

Even though he wasn't carrying his power, he was still the god of death. People tended to pay attention to him when he was in a room.

"Will there be tea?" he asked.

"Every kind I can get my hands on," I said.

"Will we receive preferred booking status?"

"Yes. This is ours first before anyone else."

He turned his head just enough that I could see him in partial profile. "Will you book this space to the Scrabblers?"

His voice had this tone to it. Like each word was a stone being dropped into a deep, dark well.

"No Scrabblers allowed!" Xtelle announced. "They are our sworn enemies. We will not allow those people to disgrace our beloved space. We will draw the line and fight them at every turn! Guards here—" she trotted to the end of the hall, "—and in the towers! Tile by tile, double letter or triple word, we shall not let them pass!"

She galloped back into the room and struck a pose, her nose in the air, her tail swishing.

"I heard they have a new member," Fawn drawled. She was leafing through a leatherbound book she'd pulled off the shelf.

"Oh?" Sage asked, playing along. "Who could that be?"

"I'll let you guess. I heard she almost started a war in the group by using an illegal word."

"No one believes that," Xtelle snipped. "Qi is *not* illegal! It is a perfectly acceptable alternate spelling for chi. They're all just a bunch of babies."

"You?" I said. "You're playing Scrabble with the Scrabblers? The goons? Your sworn enemies?"

"Who said I was playing Scrabble? As if I, Xtelle, would lower myself to…"

"You lost," Than announced.

Xtelle spun toward him. "Shut your lying pie hole. I took home twelve dollars. Twelve."

"Let's vote," Dusi interrupted. "All who want this beautiful new space, raise your hands. Or hoof."

Every hand (and, hey, even one hoof) went up.

"Yay!" Piper clapped.

"Wonderful!" I said. "We need to choose a day when we can all get together…"

Xtelle trotted over to the love seat and jumped up onto the soft cushions. She craned her head back, bit the corner of her cape, and shook, causing the material to smooth out over her neck and shoulders.

"I declare and call to order an emergency meeting of the Group of Ordinary Book Enthusiasts and Readers," she said. "Take a seat. I have important business to address."

Fawn shut the book with a thump. "We already voted, Xtelle. We're not going to read your cozy supernatural horse murder mystery."

"Trilogy!" Xtelle said. "And it is not a murder mystery. It is a mystery about murder."

"Overruled," Sage said. "Did you hear Fawn? We already voted. The vote on that book was no."

"But mysteries about *murder*," she whined.

Than turned away from the window but didn't step further into the room. Sunlight and hard shadows carved him into a foreboding figure.

Only his T-shirt which had the Schoolhouse Rock train conductor on it and read: "AND BUT AND ORDINARY… will get you pretty far," ruined the vibe.

"Are there other emergency items to attend to?" he asked.

Xtelle leveled a full glare at him, her eyes extra narrow.

Not going to lie, it made her look a little deranged.

"Yes," she said. "Who will bring the snacks to the next meeting? And none of those weird-flavored Oreo cookies. Harvest Basket isn't a flavor."

"I'll do it," Delta said. "I have a couple brownie recipes I want to try."

"Fine," Xtelle said. "Meeting adjourned."

She threw her head back against the couch. "You people are so difficult," she complained to the ceiling. "I don't know why I bother so much."

"You could bother us less," Sage offered.

I snickered, and Fawn grinned.

"Well, today we have a full box of Puffin Muffin pastries," I said. "Anyone want to stay for a bite?"

"Me." Fawn threw her hand up.

"I'll hang for a bit," Herman said.

I knew Dusi and Piper were staying because we were

going to go over our schedules and plans for getting the Rookery ready to open to the public.

"Are they chocolate?" Xtelle asked.

"Some of them are," I said.

"Fine. Bring me a soda."

"Drinks are right over there." I pointed. "Than? I'd love your input on the plans for the place. Can you take some time and stay awhile?"

He gave me a steady stare. He didn't smile (he never smiled), but I could see a glint of humor in his eyes. "I am Death, Jules Larkwood. I can take all the time I need."

Q

THE VAMPIRE SHOWED UP AROUND SUNSET. HE COULD GO OUT in the daylight—all vampires could—but Ordinary made it easier than normal for him to do so.

I think he came by my shop that late just to be dramatic.

"Closing?" he asked as he breezed through the doorway. He was wearing loose linen pants, slides, and a baggy sweater in a rust color that did good things to his complexion and dark hair.

"Yep," I said. "For the night. But pretty soon, it will be for good."

He tipped his head, as if he could hear something, maybe that mind-to-mind thing vampires could do, and a small smile curved his lips.

"Sage told me you inherited the Rookery and you're moving shop."

"I am. All the crystals and Tarot and other items. Well, most of them. Marty's going to take over this space and expand it into a board game café, but he wants a little of the Fool Moon left here. I think he's going to turn it into something wonderful."

"It's always been wonderful." He gazed at the shop as if seeing the future. "But like I said before, a game café would really add something to Ordinary."

"It will," I agreed. "You're here about the bet, aren't you?"

"First, I want to hear all the gory details. Was there a murder?"

"Yes. How did you know that was going to happen? I mean, you came into my shop just before Burgess was dug up—that's a pretty big coincidence."

Rossi spread his hands. "I was here when he died. I always wondered if his death was more than an accident. But I had no idea he'd be reanimated so many years later."

"So it was just a coincidence you made the bet?

"Do you think I can see the future?"

"No."

"Do you think I was somehow in the murderer's confidence?"

I paused for an extra beat which earned me a bigger smile from him.

"No. If you had known what Clara was doing, you'd have told Delaney so you could win the bet."

He tapped his temple. "Do you think that maybe, over all these years I've been alive *and* all the years I've been in Ordinary, that I can make a fair assumption that, eventually, there will be crimes, and that you, curious, helpful Jules, will be in the middle of trying to solve them?"

"I don't try to solve all the crimes in Ordinary."

"No, but you do want to help everyone. You're a smart, warm, welcoming person. You care for this town, and you care for the people in the town. When a crime happens, you always want to help. It's your nature."

"So even making the bet was a bet?"

"Let's just say that I'm patient. I knew a crime would happen eventually. That it happened so soon? All the better for me."

"Except you lost."

"Did I?"

"I found Burgess undead before Delaney. I found Marlene before anyone else. I figured out West was kidnapped before anyone else."

"Is that all? The bet was you'd find the killer before Delaney."

"I did! I went to Clara's house and down into that basement and had everything under control before Delaney showed up."

"Clara was the killer?"

"She wanted immortality."

He was still a moment, and I had some time to think about how many centuries he'd watched parade by. He leaned in just a bit like sharing a secret. "Immortality isn't worth killing for."

"Oh, I agree. But she didn't see it that way. She was

willing to kill us all, bring us back to life, and re-kill us for good to get her shot at immortality."

"How selfish," he said, which made me laugh.

"Well, that's one way to look at it. But it means I won our bet. So, pay up."

"Fair." He offered his hand. "Come with me, and you can choose any stone you wish."

"From your secret vault."

"From my secret vault."

"Which you haven't messed with to take out the most valuable stones."

"I have some sense of honor, you know."

"Say it."

"The vault where I haven't removed the most valuable stones, because why would I expect to lose?"

I came out from behind the counter. "Because you underestimated me."

"I did not. I never have."

"Can I ask a question?"

"Sure."

"Why do you want that old compact mirror anyway?"

"Have you opened it?" he asked.

"Yes."

"Have you opened it around a vampire?"

"No."

"Try it sometime."

"I will."

"By the way," he said. "I like the new look. Are you going to stick with it for a while?"

I knew he was talking about me looking my age, or at least closer to it, with my silvered hair and wrinkles.

"Yes," I said. "Maybe for a long, long time."

Q

WANT TO READ MORE FROM DEVON?

Find her latest books and fun newsletter at her website: www.devonmonk.com

ACKNOWLEDGMENTS

Let's get to the juicy gossip first. Yes, there really was a Scrabble club in my town, and yes, they stole our writing group's meeting room at the library!

I have no hard feelings, but I did think those wily Scrabblers would make an amusing foe for Ordinary's little book club. So in the book they went!

Our lovely witch, Jules Larkwood first showed up in GODS AND ENDS, book 3 of the Ordinary Magic series. I hadn't really planned to put her in the book, but there she was, showing me Delaney and her sisters had an auntie figure to help take care of them when their mother died.

I instantly loved Jules' warm heart, easy laugh, and big personality so I was very excited to get to know her better in GORGON WITH THE WIND, book 1 of the Ordinary Oregon Mystery series.

Now she gets her own book, and I had so much fun with her. I hope you've enjoyed spending some time with her too!

This book never would have come about if not for my delightful author friend, Liz Hartley's staunch belief in it and me. Thank you for being such a wonderful check-in buddy!

My thanks to the amazing cover artist Lyn Forester, who really nailed the fun and witchy tone of the book.

To Sharon Elaine Thompson, thank you for your incredibly quick and thorough copy edit. You rock!

To my Husband Russ, my kiddos Kameron, Mike, Konner, Anna (and Phoebe!) thank you for letting me be a part of your lives. You are certainly the best part of mine. I love you.

Big thank you to my Patreon friends, Aleta Goin, Alice Hickcox, TJ Thorton, Anne Tisdale, and many others. You have no idea how much your support means to me.

Lastly, but never least, thank you, my dear reader, for coming to visit Ordinary for a spell. I hope you had a laugh, got a chance to relax, and hang out with a few old and new friends. Come on back any time! Ordinary will always be here for you!

ALSO BY DEVON MONK

ORDINARY MAGIC

Death and Relaxation

Devils and Details

Gods and Ends

Rock Paper Scissors

Dime a Demon

Hell's Spells

Sealed With A Tryst/At Death's Door

Nobody's Ghoul

Brute of All Evil

Dues and Don'ts (newsletter sign up only)

SOULS OF THE ROAD

Wayward Souls

Wayward Moon

Wayward Sky

Wayward Devils

Wayward Gods

Wayward Vows

MYSTIC CROSSROADS

Oak and Ink

Willow and Stars - TBA

Pine and Bone - TBA

ORDINARY OREGON MYSTERY

Gorgon with the Wind

For Whom the Spell Tolls

A Seer and Present Danger

HOUSE IMMORTAL

House Immortal

Infinity Bell

Crucible Zero

BROKEN MAGIC

Hell Bent

Stone Cold

Back Lash

Dirty Work

LAS FABLES MYSTERY

Nursery Crimes

WEST HELL MAGIC

Hazard

Spark

AGE OF STEAM

Dead Iron - TBA

Tin Swift - TBA

Cold Copper - TBA

ALLIE BECKSTROM - TBA

Magic to the Bone

Magic in the Blood

Magic in the Shadows

Magic on the Storm

Magic at the Gate

Magic on the Hunt

Magic on the Line

Magic without Mercy

Magic for a Price

SHORT FICTION

A Cup of Normal (collection)

One Foolish Joy - TBA

ABOUT THE AUTHOR

Devon Monk is a National Bestselling fantasy author. She loves magic, action, hope, and people getting their happily ever afters. So it's no surprise her books are brimming with heart, humor, and people you want to cheer for. She writes short stories (they have magic too!) which can be found in various anthologies and in her collection: *A Cup of Normal*.

She lives happily beneath the rainy skies of Oregon. When not writing, she can be found drinking too much coffee, watching hockey, and knitting adorable little toys.